Unc

Something is missing…can Chet find a woman he could let himself love? Can he take the chance on something his childhood has shown him won't work, something that could mess up the peace he's found at Sunrise Ranch?

Sunrise Ranch, a foster home to many boys like Chet Grall, had been and always would be the place he now calls home. Grown, he's remained on the ranch as the top ranch hand to the McDermott brothers—his brothers here where his new life began. But after watching all three of them marry, there's a hollow spot inside him, a spot he's trying to ignore.

April Mallory lives a life all to herself. A much-loved fiction writer—under a pen name; no one knows who she is or her real name—her entire life has been lived in hiding. Though there is no longer a need to hide, she has remained a person who keeps to herself. But now, she's come to Dew Drop, Texas, to meet Mabel, a reader whose letter to April—actually, to her writing name—has intrigued April. Not that she will reveal to the inn owner who she is, but she couldn't help but come check out the Sunrise Ranch, the home for foster kids that Mabel has written to her about.

She's here for research, nothing more. But she doesn't count on a flood, getting swept away and being rescued by a cowboy—a cowboy who immediately took her breath away and made her heart pound like never, ever before.

She'll keep her secrets and then move on…but can she? Mabel had been right when she'd said meeting the boys at Sunrise Ranch would be life-changing, because Chet is one of those foster boys; he's just all grown up. The stunning cowboy has put her world into an undeniable spin.

Can she overcome her past and let love take over? Will the boys and ladies of Dew Drop help make another match of hearts

UNDENIABLE COWBOY

Cowboys of Dew Drop, Texas, Book Four

DEBRA CLOPTON

Undeniable Cowboy

Copyright © 2022 Debra Clopton Parks

CHAPTER ONE

Turbulent rain had begun as if God had just lifted the floodgates and Author April Mallory gripped the steering wheel of the small Mercedes, a two-seater that was way too low to the ground on this country road. Vicious and unforgiving rain poured down around her as she headed toward the tiny town of Dew Drop, Texas.

Why, *oh* why, had she taken this tiny, almost nonexistent road on the map when she could have gone on a much better, busier road?

Because she'd wanted to see part of the Sunrise Ranch, that was why.

Bad move was all she could say, because she'd seen the storm clouds but assumed she could make it to the small town before it started. And she hadn't expected the entire sky to bust open and every drop imaginable to pour down upon her. What was greeting her now was so far from being a "dew drop" that she could barely think. The pounding on the glass from the rain was loud, reminding her that this car was made for city roads, not back country roads like this one. A road made for flooding, from the looks of it.

She had just reached a small bridge that had water starting to cross it. Thankfully, it hadn't been deep yet but it had been tricky on the tires as she slid a bit. She lifted her foot from the gas, grasping the wheel as her tires regained their grip and she got the car back under control.

Thank goodness.

The problem was she was headed downhill and knew from the map on her phone another bridge was at the end of this downhill slope. She needed to make it across that before more water rose above the bridge; it was a lot lower down this hill, so she would be lucky if she reached it and could get across it. Water was building up, as best she could see through the downpour, all along the pastures she was passing. The ditches were filled to the brim and before long, most of this land would be covered. If it were just a hydroplane situation, she had trained to do as she'd just done; it had worked but this was about to be a pure flood.

Focus. Continuing to grip the steering wheel,

2

fighting to keep the car steady, she reminded herself that she might use this experience later on in a book. She often used things that happened around her, even bad things.

She needed to get to that second bridge quickly. She lightly pressed the gas pedal and, thankfully, her tires held their grip. Soon she'd reach the bridge, cross it, and head into Dew Drop.

The town intrigued her—had for the last couple of months since she'd received a letter from Mabel Tilsbee, the Dew Drop Inn owner. Mabel had written to B.P. Joel, the name April wrote under, about Dew Drop and also the large ranch on the outskirts of town that was a foster home for sixteen boys at a time. Mabel told how not all kids in foster care hated it like April's main character did.

Some benefited from it; yes, for some it was a wonderful experience. April knew this was true, but not for her. She hadn't benefited from the ones she'd passed through. Thank goodness she'd taken control after being released on her own and she'd become a successful author.

Thus, here she was, driving this fancy car that she was wishing right now was a huge SUV with strong tires and a lot more height from the ground than this small, close to the ground, Mercedes.

Don't think about that right now—focus on getting to Dew Drop.

Getting there in one piece and meeting this lady who had intrigued her with her letter about her town and the foster kids at Sunrise Ranch.

The town sounded lovely, and the people did too: Miss Jo, who owned the Spotted Cow Café. Mabel, owner of the Dew Drop Inn. And their buddy Nana, one of the founders of the Sunrise Ranch foster home for boys.

She took her gaze off the road for a second and tried to look through the downpour at what she thought was the ranch on either side of her. That was the reason she'd chosen this shortcut to Dew Drop—so she could see the ranch, or a part of it, anyway. It wasn't the best view because the rain and clouds were covering it up. But she knew there were pasture land, trees, and a lot of cattle. Cattle that were probably cuddled up together or hiding in the trees. Or rolling around in the mud...who knew.

Hopefully, they weren't on this road so she wouldn't have to worry about running into one.

All this aside, she'd been drawn to this town, and so she'd come and was looking forward to exploring. Doing some research and enjoying herself...and maybe use some of what she saw in her work.

She reached the bridge. It was deeper than she

wanted it to be, but thankfully it was short so, thinking she could make it across she kept going. Water roared up on both sides of the car, like she was skiing through it on a single water ski. Her eyes locked onto the thick rain ahead of her, she said a brief prayer and gripping the steering wheel she kept going.

Finally, she reached the other side of the bridge then suddenly the feel of the road beneath her tires changed and her car yanked to the left, slid toward the water-filled ditch then to the right—she was not in control. The car hydroplaned across the road, bounced onto the watery weeds and she knew she was in trouble as the car spun around like an ice-skater in an Olympic competition, jumped and then headed down the slope toward the rushing river—and the barbwire fence with heavy wooden poles barely sticking up out of the water.

She gasped, knowing the water could—no, *would* sweep her downstream.

Oh boy, this was *not* how she'd envisioned her trip.

She was in trouble.

Big, deep, rushing trouble.

* * *

Chet Grall drove through the stormy weather on a back road that cut through the lowest section of the ranch.

Sunrise Ranch, the place he called home ever since he'd been through an ordeal with his family that had made him a boy with no home and no family. He hadn't enjoyed being abandoned when it first happened, and foster homes kept letting him go. He'd just been too mangled inside to handle his ordeal. Then, two years after being that hard-to-handle, hurting kid, he'd ended up here at Sunrise Ranch, with the three boys who'd lost their mother. The amazing woman whose dream it had been to open their humongous ranch as a foster home for boys who weren't as lucky to be loved like her boys were with a mother, a father, and a grandmother who adored them.

But those boys had lost their mother when she'd died of cancer, but their grandmother and their dad had picked up her dream, opening Sunrise Ranch to sixteen boys who had no place to call home and no loved ones to help. Boys whose problems and attitudes many times were as torn up and rough as his had been. This made other places not right for them. Thus, here he was, calling it home, and he loved all the people who had embraced him and helped him make it through his struggles. He still had some, but he didn't talk about them; he didn't focus on them. No, he focused on the ranch and helping the boys as they came to know that life could go on if they could make it through the trauma, the problems they were left struggling with when they came here.

This ranch was the place to lose yourself in all that went on: the cattle drives, the horses, donkey escapes, roundups, and rodeos—all but bull riding. Bull riding was off-limits, though one fella had made it onto the college rodeo team with his bull riding ability. Thinking about Wes made him smile. He was a success story, and he'd honored the no-bull-riding rule on the ranch but had learned it on another place and was doing great. Everyone was happy for him. And though Chet hadn't said anything, he'd known the boy was riding but also knew Wes was driven to ride.

Bull riding to that young man had been a release of internal pain and enabled him to be a leader of all the boys on the ranch through his years here. Wes had put a cover on his deep emotions and found a way to deal with them, therefore able to be there for all the younger kids around him. Chet had done the same thing Wes was doing now: pushed the things he couldn't control into the deep corners of his brain and heart and then found his footing here on this great ranch. The place he planned to grow old on…home.

This was Chet's home now and always would be.

Most everyone who'd come here had moved on with their lives after leaving; many were happily married and living great lives. There were others who hadn't been able to cross the line of falling in love and getting married.

He was one of them—still, he was able to focus on helping the boys who came to Sunrise Ranch make it through the rough beginnings and adapt to the good life here on the ranch. He'd especially enjoyed the last little while, watching the young ones see Morgan, Rowdy, and Tucker find love and marry.

He'd been glad each of them had seen what life could be like when they found the right woman to love and found their happily-ever-afters. They'd seen that love could make it through hard times and that they could be chosen to love—like Jolie, the great competitive kayaker who had chosen to give that up for her love of Morgan and for them too.

She'd chosen them over kayaking competition despite how good and how much she'd loved it—chosen teaching them at the ranch's school, showing them her love. She was their mother; as were Lucy, Rowdy's wife, and Suzie, Tucker's wife.

The boys, most of them, were doing great and that made him happy. His brothers had brought wonderful women into the lives of his smaller brothers and for that he was grateful. But him, nope. And on that thought he went back to concentrating on his job.

He made sure that the fence lines were okay. That they had no cattle getting out. No cattle struggling in the water that was starting to rise over the bridges and making passage hard. This was the low side of the ranch and nothing ever happened that was bad, but he always came just to make sure no unsuspecting drivers were caught. He knew from personal experience that it just took one time to change lives—like his had been changed that night all those years ago.

He saw something ahead of him through the rain in his large-wheeled four-wheel-drive truck high off the ground, which could handle the overflow of the bridges. But as he headed downhill, he saw lights. Red lights close to the railing of the bridge he knew was at the bottom of the hill. The lights flickered as the car moved slowly. The car, he could tell, was probably too stinkin' low to the ground to make it across that bridge. The water was flowing fast, and he knew it from the last bridge; this one was far lower than that one had been. He pressed the gas, and drove faster than he should to cut the distance between him and whoever was in that car.

As he made it almost to the bridge, he watched the car reach the other side. Watched helplessly as it hydroplaned, swerved one way, and then caught the draft of water and shot across the road into the downhill slide of the grass before hitting another obstacle that spun it out of control down the hill. Directly toward the raging water that had overtaken the bridge.

There were no good options. It would hit the water, slam into the bridge, and then probably be beneath it. And then it'd only get worse...just like what had happened to his parents and him. Only he'd lived, thanks to a man who had fought through the water to rescue him the next morning as he clung alone to a small tree in the raging water. His parents had been nowhere in sight.

Not happening tonight. Chet stomped the gas, held onto the steering wheel, and prayed he'd make it across to help whoever was in that car.

Moments later, he was across the bridge, his gigantic wheels on solid ground in the rushing water that had swept the tiny car into danger. He pressed the brakes and halted on the pavement as he slammed the gear into park and threw himself from the cab. Adrenaline pumping, he raced through the now nearly knee-high water to the far side of the bridge. Then he stormed as firmly as he could through the deepening water, heading down the hill toward the car. The car that—thank the good Lord—had hit a fence post that was barely showing in the water. He knew because he'd helped build it that barbed wire was attached to the fence post.

This strong fence kept cattle from entering the river on a good day, not to hold a car while water fought to suck it downstream. Nope, this wasn't in the game book—and it was clear that it wouldn't hold the small car for long, but at least it gave him a chance to get to the driver.

He threw himself toward the car, grabbed hold of the fender, and then reached for the door handle on the driver's side. Thank goodness he was tall and was only chest-high in the water. He looked in the window and met the startled, wide eyes of a woman who was struggling to push the door open but clearly having no success. So, he joined in and instantly knew on this side it was never going to happen. The rushing water blasted him and the car as he fought to pull the door open against the raging water. He realized as he pulled that too much pressure was against them. Determined, he let go, pulled himself back and around to the other side, where the water swirled around him but the pressure was less as he yanked on the door. Thank goodness, it opened, and he placed his body between the door and the inside of the car; then he held his hand out.

She just stared at him over her shoulder, still pushing against the other door.

"Come on, grab my hand and let's get you out of there," he basically yelled, worry building that the fence was going any moment. Her wide eyes glistened like light gold shining in the moonlight. *Where had that come from?* He reached farther in. "Grab hold," he urged, not so harsh.

She slapped her hand in his, and he pulled her over the console of the two-seater; she floated through the water into his arms.

He held her tightly as she looked up at him. Instantly, his heart pounded as he met that gold gaze, he froze. But only for a moment, they didn't have long in the water as it pulled and pushed, swirling powerfully around them. But even in that small segment of time, he knew he'd never seen eyes like hers. Eyes that dug deep and attached to him with sparkling hope, lifting him up as he tightened his arm around her and gritted out, "Hang on."

She did exactly that: her arms clung to him as he stepped back, away from the car, and the full force of the raging water slammed into them.

The water churned harder against them as he fought his way through the rough flowing river uphill, toward safety. He had to get just a few steps, *stay steady*— which wasn't easy as the water fought against them and he fought to stay up, something he only ever had to do before in a major wrestle with a bull. Which was something he rarely had to do. But right now, he was holding a sparkling golden-eyed female whose life depended on him, and he would not let her down.

As they made it to the edge where the water lost traction, her grip tightened around his neck, and his around her waist. He paused and took a deep breath, staring into those eyes. He had exerted a lot and couldn't say much, but she clung so tightly to him. Her eyes hung onto him as tightly as her arms were, and her legs had wrapped around his waist. Yeah, she was hanging on tight. He took a deep breath, trying to find the words to tell her it was going to be okay.

"Thank you," she gasped, before he could speak, and then she kissed him—her lips locked onto his, her arms squeezed him tighter—and lightning shot through him like the bolts cracking through the surrounding sky.

His knees weakened, and he was thankful he stood on steady ground—then his boots slipped out from under him and they both fell into the now shallow water.

CHAPTER TWO

What am I doing?

When they hit the ground, mud splattered around them. Her brain had started working the instant they landed in the shallow water and *thank goodness* her lips disconnected from her hero.

No, not her hero. *No, no, no*—the man who had…saved her from what had almost been her last moments of life if he hadn't gotten her out of that car.

She was breathing hard as she stared at the man who looked as if he were in just as much shock as she was from her behavior. *Okay, girl, get a grip.*

Deep breath. "Sorry, that's not my usual reaction, but okay, thank you for rescuing me. I will forever be in your debt. I know I was almost a goner. I could see that before you came along, and your bravery—goodness, you didn't even think. You just came into that water and took me out of that situation…wow. Thank you." She gasped in a breath. "But please don't be bothered by my kiss. That was not a normal response, but honestly, I've never been in that situation. Never had a cowboy—no, a hero pull me out like that. So, thank you. I'm forever grateful."

She was rattling away with things she shouldn't say, and he was just lying there in the water, still holding her and looking at her like she was a—what, a crazy woman? He looked as if he were stunned.

Water flowed around him but not over him. Breathing hard, she patted him on the chest. "Are you okay? Please tell me you're okay. Tell me you didn't rescue me like that and now you're hurt, because I don't know what I'm going to do."

She was freaking out again. She was losing it.

"I'm…fine. I'm glad you're okay." He sucked in a breath. "Honestly, I'm just happy I was here. Sorry I'm reacting like this. Here, let me help you get up. Just to let you know, I lost my mom and dad in a river accident when I was a young kid. I've never had to rescue someone but I'm very pleased I was here for you. No one was around or able to rescue my parents but I somehow washed out of the car and ended up clinging to a tree all night until a man came in after me the next morning. He threw himself into the water and pulled me out in a similar way, so I kind of know what you're thinking." And then his lips lifted into a gentle, knowing smile.

Oh goodness, her already pounding heart shifted in a very unusual way. No, she never reacted that way—it had to do with the way he'd spoken of his parents. That was it. "I'm so overjoyed you were here for me but I'm very sorry no one was there for your parents. But thankful the wonderful man was there for you."

"I've adjusted to it over the years, but that's one reason here on the ranch, when it floods like this, I always come here to the lowest area. I'm checking on cattle, making sure fences I've helped build are doing their job. Like the one that caught your car. But honestly, I'm always thinking about that moment in my life when I was too young to help. The moment I saw your taillights, I knew I had to get to you. I'm driven to help, not wanting what happened to me to happen to anyone else. So, thankfully, my ordeal had me here to help you."

What a story... Her mind churned as the man slid her off the top of him, then rose to a standing position then pulled her up out of the shallow water. Her brain had started working overtime at his words, his sad story.

Her thoughts rolled, going over what he'd said—*my*

ordeal had me here to help you.

Her mind reeled as he took her arm and headed up the last of the incline, then toward a large truck sitting in what was the road below the foot of water surrounding it. The huge, big-wheeled truck would not go off the pavement like her tiny car had done.

"I see you came prepared." Her gaze moved from his truck to look up at him.

"Yeah, that is a cattle truck but it's more for the back roads and gullies. I ride a lot of horses down into the gullies but, still, that truck comes in handy." He pulled open the door and then, to her surprise, he scooped her into his arms, and gently placed her in the seat.

Once again, she was stunned as their gazes locked. *Wow.* She thought about that kiss that should have never happened. "I guess I'll buckle up. I'm sorry I'm getting the inside of your truck wet."

"Don't worry about it. This truck and leather seats have carried a lot of animals, many dusty or muddy cowboys, and now you. I'll wipe it out when we get to town. Buckle up."

With those words, he stepped back and closed the door and gave her a few moments to get her head on straight. To stop thinking about the kiss and the storyline racing through her creative brain. Her life was all about storylines, and as she buckled up, she watched him stride around the front of the truck and she tried to relax. Tried to remind herself this was real life.

This was not a storyline.

This was the real deal.

But...this is a real hero.

Not an invented one in your head.

As he climbed into the truck, her heart pounded harder.

Thankfully, finally, he buckled up and placed one hand on the steering wheel then the other on the gearshift. "Okay, here we go. I'm taking you to Dew Drop. I have a feeling that's where you were headed, since that's the only place anywhere near the end of this road."

"Yes, Dew Drop is exactly where I was going. I have a reservation at the Dew Drop Inn."

"That's where I am heading." His eyes twinkled—making her heart do a jig. "That's a great place to go. And Mabel would take care of you whether you were staying there or not. By the way, I'm Chet Grall." He held out his hand and gave her a smile.

She looked at his hand, hesitated then slipped hers into his. "And I'm a very grateful April Mallory."

"And I'm very glad to meet you." Then he let go of her hand, took the steering wheel, pushed the gas pedal, and the truck began to move through the low-lying water. Water that was much better to get out of than get into.

Her gaze caught on him; she no longer had to force that kiss and what she'd been through out of her head. No, her head was now spinning with story ideas and she knew good and well that nothing stopped that when it started.

CHAPTER THREE

Chet pulled into the main street of Dew Drop, relieved to see the sign on the front of the steadfast Dew Drop Inn shining through the thick rain. Mabel was dedicated to making the place wonderful, and he completely appreciated it at this moment.

He glanced over at his passenger. "Mabel will take care of you, and even if you don't have anything to wear, I'm sure she'll find you something. There's a store down the street that can help you out too. Or I could also ask my sisters-in-laws if they have something you can wear—"

"No, I'm fine, thank you. I can buy more clothes after I get my purse back or have new cards overnighted. But hopefully she'll have a washer and dryer I can use tonight and I'll be able wear these tomorrow. But about my car…"

"Don't worry about your car." He pulled into the parking space in front of the inn. "We'll get it out. If the fence and the tree hold it. But can't do that until this downpour moves on. I won't risk anyone going in after a car—coming in after you was a different story—"

"I totally agree. I don't want anyone to risk getting hurt or worse. What I lose, I lose. I'm very grateful that you came in after me and always will be. Everything else is just stuff. Even my computer and my work is nothing."

"You work on your computer?"

"Yes, but everything is backed up. I can buy a new one and be fine."

"I'm sorry. Do you need one right now?"

She shook her head. "No, I can do without it for a few days. I'm alive, and that's what's important. Thank you again for coming in after me."

He stared at her beautiful golden eyes and was thankful he'd been there. God's timing had saved her, not him.

He didn't think her car was still hanging onto the fence. The currents got deeper and the car was now floating far downstream, somewhere stuck in a tree or under a tree after it had been swept downstream. Floods were no joke, but he didn't want to let her know right now how much of a dire situation she'd been in. He'd deal with that tomorrow after she was dry, probably well fed and pampered by the lady he was about to take her in and introduce her to.

"Let's get out and go inside. Mabel will take good care of you and over there at the Spotted Cow Café—or as many jokingly call it, the Cow Pattie Café—Miss Jo will feed you good. Mabel's room service comes from the Cow Pattie." He grinned at the joke, and she did too.

"They sound nice." She reached for the door handle.

"Hold on, wait for me. I'll come help you out. I don't want to take the chance that you slip and hit your head on the concrete after what we went through to get you out of that flood." Without waiting for her to say anything, he had his door opened and shut behind him as he stepped into the rain and hurried around the end of the truck and then pulled her door open.

"Wow," she said, a smile of disbelief on her pretty face. "You're a go-getter."

He grinned. "At your service, ma'am." He held out his hand.

There was water covering the pavement and drenching him—but they were both already soaked, so what was a little more? With only a hesitation, looking at his hand, she slid hers into his.

Lightning shot through him again. *What in the*

dickens was this?

Her eyes had flown wide, making him pretty certain she'd felt something too.

This was ridiculous.

He wasn't looking for lightning bolts or being drawn to those beautiful eyes, golden sparkles that were wide with—*horror*?

Oh wow, he needed to shove all this to the back of his thoughts. "I've got you," he said, encouragingly, like he would say to an injured cow or a newborn who needed his help. "Let's get you inside so you can get comfortable." And he meant in more ways than comfortable with Mabel. It was clearly obvious that she was not comfortable with him. Then again, he was feeling overwhelmed himself.

Distance—that was what they both needed. To get dry. They were both soaked, not to mention traumatized. They needed to get their heads on straight.

Holding her hand, he led her to the steps and up onto the sidewalk just as the inn's front door flew open and there stood Mabel.

A tall woman with broad shoulders and a smile that could wipe away a raging storm and eyes that danced as they took in the two of them. "Oh, my goodness, y'all come on inside. Chet, what in the world happened?"

"Mabel, this is April Mallory. She got caught in the

flooding down on the low road."

"Oh dear, come on inside and let's get you two dry."

He took hold of the door so Mabel could lead the way into the inn, and then he motioned with his free hand for April to go ahead before him. Their gazes met briefly before she followed the rapidly talking Mabel inside.

"I recognize the name, April, from booking your room. I'm so glad to have you and so sorry for what you've been through. Now, you just come on in and don't you worry, everything is ready. We're going to get you to your room so you can clean up. I'll take those wet clothes of yours, and wash them for you. Don't worry, there's a housecoat in the room waiting for you. You tell me what you'd like to eat, and I'll have it brought over so you can relax. A nice, warm luxury bath can be yours if you'd rather have that than a shower. I believe you'll enjoy it since you've been through this horrible ordeal. Just unwind, okeydokey?"

Chet grinned at the look of astonishment on April's face from the nonstop words of fixing everything she could fix. That was Mabel. "I told you she would take care of you." It was true; the sweet lady took mission trips all over the place to help people.

"I'm certainly going to do my best. And my buddy

Jo across the street at the Spotted Cow Café can cook out of this world, so I know you're going to love whatever you choose off the menu in your room. I use her awesome cooking as an excuse not to have a diner in the hotel. I could never do anything to compare to her masterpieces." She leaned toward April with a grin. "The truth is, I'm just not interested in cooking, so Jo and I have a special friendship."

They all laughed, and he enjoyed the dancing of April's amazing golden eyes.

"It sounds like the two of you were meant to be," April said, still chuckling.

He loved it—loved watching the play between the two ladies. Nothing more. Just their cute interaction.

"True, on so many levels. You're going to love it, I promise. Her special of the day is chicken pot pie with cheese on top, a town favorite."

"That sounds wonderful. I would love it, and everything you're saying sounds amazing. I really appreciate it." She looked at him again. "But what about you? Are you going to be okay?"

"I'll be fine. As long as you are. I know you're in excellent hands, so I'll head back to the ranch. I'll take a hot shower, put on some clean, *dry* clothes, and relax for the evening. I'm pretty sure there won't be anyone else out on that bridge today." He forced a smile because he didn't want her seeing how worried he'd been about the whole situation.

"I think that is a great plan." Mabel smiled at both of them. "It's been a rough day for both of y'all. Getting dry and relaxing will be good for you both. Chet, you come back tomorrow so you and April, can get reintroduced in a much less risky way." She grinned widely, looking from him to April.

The lady had a sense of humor. She knew this had been a horrible experience, so she was helping ease it up. He stepped back and lifted his hand to tip his hat, only then remembering his Stetson was floating down the stream after being washed from his head at some point. It was actually the first time he'd thought about it, hadn't even realized it had come off until this moment. He'd had a hat on when he'd entered that water with only one thing on his mind: rescuing whoever was in the car.

Relief washed through him again. He had another hat at the house and he'd rather lose a million or more hats any day than lose someone to that water. Meeting her golden, penetrating eyes, he was very glad he'd been there for her. Now, he needed to get out of here.

"Sounds like a good plan. I'll check on you tomorrow. But don't worry, I won't be getting in your way. Like Mabel said, it will be nice to meet under different circumstances. Welcome to Dew Drop. It's usually more welcoming than the way it welcomed you." That got a smile. And he liked it.

On that note, he turned and headed to the door as his wet boots made a thundering noise on the wooden floors of the hotel. He didn't slow down as he pulled the door closed behind him and stalked straight to his truck. He climbed inside as quick as possible because he wasn't exactly sure what he was thinking.

It was time to get home and get real.

* * *

"Now, just follow me up these stairs and give me those dirty clothes, and I'll take care of them while you shower or take a hot bath. Also, tell me what you'd like to eat—there is a menu on the table and I'll have it brought over for you."

April almost laughed at the tone and the grin Mabel gave her. "I can't wait to try the food. I'd just as soon eat a peanut butter sandwich rather than cook."

"Now we're talkin'. But I promise you, once you eat Jo's food, you'll want it over the sandwich. Like I said earlier her special today is chicken pot pie."

"That sounds wonderful. I would love it. I really appreciate all you're doing." The bathtub would have felt great with so many wonderful choices of bath oils but she decided to take a shower instead. The pressure from the waterspout was wonderful and the pressure of it massaging her neck and shoulders helped ease some of the stress still hanging on after her afternoon. She let the hot water run through her hair, down her neck and spread across her shoulders as she thought about what nearly happened. She would never be able to thank the heroic cowboy for what he had done.

She felt better; she was alive…she had made it and all because of the nice cowboy.

She was just glad to be standing here now, drying her hair in this lovely hotel. She put on the robe; it was very soft and smelled of the wonderful scent of lavender. She sank onto the bed; so comfortable as she stretched out and took a deep breath. Her adventure to Dew Drop had not begun like she'd envisioned. But it had begun, and there was absolutely some kind of story idea that was going to come out of this. She lived it, walked it, and her brain always started working.

There was a knock on the door. She sat up and then quickly strode across the room and opened the door. There stood a woman wearing a red raincoat, red boots, and a red rain hat.

"Well, howdy, I'm Edwina. The waitress from the Spotted Cow Café." She held up a large plastic bag and grinned. "I have to tell you, I can't imagine coming through that low area in this heavy rain. I'm thankful you had that handsome cowboy, Chet, to come save you. You doin' okay?"

"Yes, I am," she said, stepping back to let her in. "I got saved by a cowboy." April's words shocked her since they sounded like she was teasing right along with Edwina.

"Yes, honey, you did," Edwina cooed and hitched her brows. "That's one good-looking cowboy that Chet is indeed. I tell you, I see a bunch of cowboys, and some of them I have to deal with in a pretty frank way. I ain't shy about words if they start getting out of hand—you know what I mean. But that Chet—well, he hasn't ever gotten out of hand, so that means you were and *are* in very good, very trustworthy hands." Edwina hitched a brow as she gave her a look, then crossed the room and set the large bag on the table by the window. "This here is the best chicken pot pie you'll ever taste. Not that I'm a professional at anything, but that's what everyone who eats it says. So, when you come into the diner tomorrow, you might tell T-bone, the chef, what you think."

"Thank you, I'll do that. Now I can't wait to try it. And, I have to ask, do you have a lot of trouble with the cowboys in town?" The woman's words had shocked her.

Edwina gave her a "are you kidding me" look. "There's no way with a herd of cowboys there's not going to be those who go out of their way to be on the wrong side of me. And believe me, after three ex-husbands, I got no problem handling them. But for the most part, this is the place to be if you're looking to find a new man and a good man. Is that what brings you to town?"

The question caught her off guard so much. "No." She laughed. "I'm here just to relax. I heard it was a quiet and great place to see the countryside." Not totally true but still somewhat true.

"Then you're in the right spot. I can guarantee it. Now, I've got to go. The café is busy, but we all wanted to make sure you had this to eat. See you tomorrow—and I don't have to say hope you enjoy the dish. I already know you will."

With that, the lady was out the door, leaving an atmosphere of positivity despite her bit of negativity.

And once again, April smiled as she hurried to the table, pulled out the dish, and lifted the lid. The scent alone had her stomach growling, and she immediately sat down, grabbed the stainless-steel fork and cloth napkin included and after placing it in her lap she lowered her head and thank God for sending Chet to save her... relief washed through her, then she thanked

Him for the food. Feeling totally and completely relieved to be here she then took a bite of the chicken pot pie—oh goodness, it was delicious.

Absolutely delicious.

This trip started out horrible, but from the moment she'd been pulled from her car, everything had been too good to be true. Not that she was going to think about everything. No, she was only going to enjoy this good food and the fact that she was alive and surrounded by what appeared to be wonderful people.

CHAPTER FOUR

Chet made it back to the ranch and despite being soaked, he drove to the main part of the property with the barns, the school, the kitchen, and across the way, the main house. He looked around just to make sure no one needed help. The lights in the little schoolhouse were off, and the lights in the house where Nana lived were all on, so he figured that was all good. He drove to the barn and saw one of the work trucks pulled close to the door. He climbed out, glad the rain had lessened, not that it mattered—he was still dripping wet so a little more wouldn't hurt.

He walked into the huge red barn and saw sixteen-year-old Tony standing at a closed stall. His jacket was wet, but not too wet, and his wavy black hair curled from beneath the edges of his rugged straw hat. The

Elvis Presley look-alike stared intently into the stall.

"Hey, Tony, what's up?"

Tony glanced at him. "I was out in the pasture, making my rounds through the expectant mama cows, and I found this little fella wandering around, barely able to walk. He was across the pasture from where the mama's and other calves were huddled together near a group of trees. He looked desperate to me, so I gathered him up and brought him here to feed. We just got here a few minutes before you. I was going over there to make him some milk and bottle feed him. I hope that's okay."

Chet smiled at the teen as he walked up and looked over the railing at the calf. It definitely looked like it needed some food. "Excellent decision. He needs feeding. I'm sorry you got caught in that storm. It's clearing up now. But I was out there too."

Tony looked at him straight on this time, his expression startled as he took in Chet's drenched appearance. "Wow, did you go swimming?"

"Well, yep, I actually did. Over there on the west side, that low road that cuts through the ranch. You know, I always go check that out if I'm suspecting the water is going to rise. And sure enough, there was a small car on the other side of the second bridge that had miraculously made it across the near foot of water covering the bridge, only to be swept down the river.

Thankfully, that fence you helped me repair caught her—the car. She was trapped inside, unable to get the doors opened. It was such a rushing high-water catastrophe, that fence wasn't going to hold that car much longer, so thankfully I make my trips and was there to get her out and to safety."

"Wow. Thank goodness you were there. What did you do with her?"

"She was on her way to the Dew Drop Inn. That's where I would have taken her no matter what, but it happened to be her destination."

"That's a great story. We both kind of saved the day today." Tony's crooked grin spread across his Elvis face.

"Yes, little brother, we did. I'm proud of you."

Tony placed a hand on his shoulder. "And *I'm* proud of you, big brother. Want to come back here and make sure I mix this cow milk replacement up correctly?"

Chet smiled at the way Tony repeated him. "Sure, and then we'll get him on a schedule. You and all your brothers will take care of him." He knew Tony accepted all the foster boys at the ranch as his brothers, just like Chet did. Sometimes it was hard on the new ones, but not Tony; he'd taken to the life on the ranch to help him get over the hard ordeals he'd been dealt. But like Chet,

Tony gladly and proudly called the ranch home, and he loved ranching.

They headed to the back wall where the counters were, and all they needed to treat the calves, cows, or horses were stored there. Tony pulled the container holding the powder and then he opened a cabinet and pulled out a measuring container. He filled it to its right measurement as Chet watched, completely certain Tony wouldn't miss a beat. And he didn't.

Once the powder was measured into the bottle, he set it on the metal shelf and weighed it. He'd learned that the density changed as the container sat there, and it always needed close attention to make sure the newborn calf got exactly what it needed. Satisfied, Tony then mixed it carefully with the prepared water, clearly understanding what he was doing—just as Chet had known he would.

After the bottle was ready, they went back to the gate. Chet opened it and followed Tony inside. The small calf lifted his head, his large eyes studying them as he looked very uneasy but too worn out to move.

"I always like this part," Tony said. "I like being a rescuer. I can't help it. We were raised here on this ranch for a good while, and you know I wasn't in great shape when I got here. But I knew a rescue when I saw it, and I needed it in a terrible way. This ranch has the right name, Sunrise—because until I got here, all I'd seen was darkness. It wasn't good. Now, here, I love waking up and watching that sun come up on a sunshiny day, a dim rainy day...any kind of day. It doesn't matter; it's a sunrise on Sunrise Ranch and it's going to be a good day." He stopped talking, his blue eyes gleaming bright and that Elvis smile lifting. "Here, I know that no matter if the sun is shining, or a storm is brewing, that *I'm* in a good place. So much better than what I was born into. And as bad as it sounds, I love it when I can rescue a baby calf and help him out. I want to help like I was helped."

Chet inhaled, holding back emotions he'd felt. He knew that feeling. It was exactly why, when many of the boys grew up they had great lives because here on this ranch the sun always shined inside their hearts always. Most everyone came back for the yearly homecoming celebration whenever they could. But he'd chosen to stay on the ranch forever, because of moments like this, watching a kid like Tony smiling and surviving. A kid who'd been through the horrible nightmare of not only being beaten, but tortured with burns...what this kid had been through was hideous...but Tony had grabbed hold of what this ranch was—a huge blessing. And he was doing great.

They all knew they owed a lot to Mr. McDermott,

his sons, and Nana, their grandmother. But it all began with the dream of Lydia McDermott. She was Morgan, Rowdy, and Tucker's mother. The sweet woman who died before her dream could come true but her family had shown their love by making sure Sunrise Ranch became exactly what she'd envisioned it to become. A place that carried out her wishes and was a blessing to all who came here.

Now, watching Tony be so determined and grateful—Chet could feel Miss Lydia smiling down on them. He'd never met her but he felt her as Tony spoke. Moments like this never stopped amazing him.

He watched as Tony let the little calf get used to the nipple on the bottle, and then Chet grinned as the calf finally figured it out and grabbed hold. Prepared for the yank, Tony was holding on tight for that moment so as not to drop the bottle when tugged by the baby, greedy for the food and nutrients it needed. The teenager bowed down beside the calf, clearly happy knowing he was helping this little fella live. That he was making a difference. It was true, but this young man wasn't just making a difference with the calves. No, he was making a difference with all the younger kids following behind him.

Chet looked at Tony. "You're doing great. You know that, don't you?"

Tony looked up at him, those deep blue eyes of his penetrating Chet's. "Thanks. I want to make a difference, just like you have. You know, I've learned a lot from Morgan, Rowdy, and Turner. But I've learned even more from you because from the little I get from your past, not that you share it that much, but I know we come from bad backgrounds and we've survived. And you, from day one, showed me what kind of man I can become. Just thought it was the right time to make that clear. Just wanted you to know I look up to you and always have."

His words hit Chet hard. "Good."

"Not just me—the others too. We know that our oldest brothers went through a lot, losing their sweet mom and having to deal with the loss of someone who loved them so much. Then their dad and grandmama, Nana, carried out Miss Lydia's dream and brought all of us here to live a better life on this amazing ranch. They had to deal with that while they were torn up inside. But now, they're still here and they seem to love all of us. I appreciate it tremendously. It's been life-changing for so many—but you... You, Chet, came into this ranch just like we did, with heartache and loss, yet you've stayed and are a success. I'm not holding it against the ones who've moved on, and found their adult lives elsewhere, not at all. But my dream is like yours. You hung out here, and I'm hoping I can do that too," he said, his eyes bright. "I'll work on this ranch like you and maybe, one day, I can open a foster ranch of my own. Anyway, just wanted to let you know."

The kid's words raced through Chet. "That right there helps me. Helps me know I made the right decision when I chose to stay here."

"Well then, I did my job saving this calf and helping you." Tony grinned. "Now, is that woman you saved okay? Is she staying at the Dew Drop Inn?"

"Yes, she is, and I'll be going tomorrow to check on her."

"Well, hey, can I go with you? I'd like to see this woman who made it across the bridge because you helped her. It's kinda cool seeing all of us who come through getting help but also seeing those we help—well, you helped. You know, others benefiting because you're here."

Chet really liked this kid. "Sure, you can go with me. I'll meet you here about ten. I don't want to bother her by getting there too early."

"I'll be here. Now, I've got this handled if you want to go home and clean up. I'm a little wet but nowhere near as soaking wet as you are. And soon as I feed this baby, I'll head back to my house. Mrs. Carrie knows what I was doing here at the barn."

"Good for you. They might be your house parents but they love you like their own, too, and they'd worry about you and all your brothers if they didn't know where you were."

"Yes, sir, I get it. I'll see you tomorrow."

Chet grinned, turned, and headed out the door. The kid had given him a clear signal he wanted to finish what he was doing alone. And it again reminded Chet of himself at that age after arriving here. He got in his truck and drove down the road toward his cabin. His mind instantly went back to that pretty April, with her cinnamon-toned brown hair and those golden sparkling eyes. And as odd as it was for him, he knew he was looking forward to seeing her again.

For a guy with no plans to ever marry, the anticipation of seeing her could cause him to make a stupid mistake.

Nope, no mistakes; she was visiting, and he was staying. And besides that, he hadn't dated in forever and had no plans to start, and everyone knew it. Rowdy had pointed out to him at Tucker's wedding that he believed Chet needed to date. But Chet knew in his heart that he could never take the chance of losing love after what he'd witnessed with his parents. He was a man who would help others, but his heart was a no go. Dating, marrying—even dancing, wasn't something he planned to do. He was a loner.

Still, he couldn't deny if he was going to test any of that out, the golden-eyed April would be the one he'd give it a shot on.

* * *

April had slept and that was highly unusual.

She hadn't slept good since the horrible loss of her parents when she was a child, after which she entered foster care and struggled with everything that had happened to her. It had been hard to understand that until the day they died, she hadn't even known her real last name. All of it had laid hard on her making her difficult to handle thus, she was passed from one home to another.

When she was a teen and at yet another foster home, troubled with the nightmares that haunted her, one night she picked up a notebook and started to write. And miraculously that had helped ease her pain and she started sleeping a bit better. And every little bit helped. It also set her on the path toward her writing career and as she put words and trauma on paper she had less nightmares about the day she'd lost her parents.

But last night—last night she'd slept *all* night. Amazing, from the moment she'd gone to sleep, about ten o'clock, until waking up here in this lovely inn about eight. It was astounding and she couldn't get over how good she felt. It was unbelievable, especially after just having nearly died in a flood.

She had survived thanks to Chet. But, not that it mattered, but her waterproof phone had also survived in her deep jeans pocket. Again, not that it mattered since she didn't have anyone to let know she'd been in the flooding river. Yes, she had acquaintances, proofers, and editors but no really close friends, and it was all her fault. She holed up and wrote or went on research trips like this one incognito and never stepped out to really get attached. She was probably the most unattached person in the world.

And she kept it that way. Now, staring up at the ceiling, she sighed. This was how it had always been, her keeping everyone at bay and no one really knowing who she really was.

So be it. She felt the soft push from deep inside to dig out of her hole. But as always she ignored it even though it was much stronger than ever before.

She was at the start of creating a new book and had all the time she wanted to research and get her ideas. She wasn't going to get a new computer right now though. She would let herself enjoy the time not typing the story out, as usual, hard and fast as if getting it out would relieve her of what drove her to write.

No, she was going to try just being here for now.

She'd make all of her notes in a notebook, which she'd need to buy at one of the stores. But, maybe she could relax and not spend all of her days typing on a computer for just a little while.

Her thoughts had gone to maybe writing a different type of book this time. Not her normal drama-filled suspense that always ended with a happy ending—the problem was solved, the bad guy or gal got what was due them and was caught or killed. For her, that was a happy ending. Basically, the heroine in the book never totally got over the losses that drove her to solve crimes and thus she never actually ended up with anyone, which would have made it a genuine romance. No, her main character always went on alone.

April knew this was her in so many ways, but writing these stories always helped her deep inside where she hid her past hurts and forced herself forward. Writing was a great helper; she just made sure no one knew it was her who wrote the stories so many people loved.

She hoped none of her readers were aching deep inside but if they were, she prayed her books helped them deal with that pain. But right now, she wasn't going to write or work, though she would get herself a notepad and take notes of inspired moments. She was going to relax, at least try to.

And if tonight, she slept as good as she slept last night, this was a huge win for her. Of course, she knew that could have only happened because she had been through a life-threatening ordeal. An ordeal with a happy ending…she was *alive* and here in this adorable place.

She'd come here to check out this ranch she had read and heard so much about and that was what she would do—and maybe even enjoy herself.

On that thought, she got out of bed. It was time to go have breakfast at the Spotted Cow Café. She dressed in her now clean and dried white jeans and pale-yellow blouse that Mabel had washed and delivered this morning. Her underwear and tennis shoes had made it too. That had been early, and she'd crawled back in bed. Mabel had also brought her a large mug of coffee and a wonderful apple fritter that she said Miss Jo kept her supplied with for early risers. The woman was awesome, but it sounded like Miss Jo was as well. And they were good friends. Mabel had encouraged her to head over to the restaurant for a wonderful late-morning breakfast, but also to experience the atmosphere she didn't want to miss.

She reached for her purse out of habit; it hadn't

been in her pocket like her phone, so she didn't have a purse or money. Mabel, the sweet lady, had told her not to worry about money, that she could charge everything to the hotel until she got a new card in the mail. And so she'd canceled all her cards and ordered new ones; they'd be here soon. All that raced through her thoughts as she headed downstairs.

Mabel had told her that she wouldn't be in but her wonderful front desk clerk, Harvey, would be and that he would help her with anything she needed. As she reached the first floor, she saw the robust older man with a thick mustache and serious eyes.

He grinned big the moment he saw her. "Good mornin'. I hope you're doing well. Miss Mabel told me to get ready to help you out with anything you needed this mornin'. I'm really glad you're safe. *And* I'm glad Chet was around to help you. That boy—well, all those boys from the ranch as they've grown up are all great. They help us out with our busy times. Chet did, too, when he was a boy. Now, anything I can do for you this mornin'?"

"Thank you. I slept great last night. It's a wonderful room and the bed was perfect. I'm heading to the café now but I'm expecting some overnighted mail sometime today, maybe this morning."

"If it comes in, I'll keep it right here for you. No

worries. You just pick them up when you have time. Now go on over there and enjoy the place. Miss Jo will take care of you."

"Thanks." She headed out the door and stepped off the sidewalk, warmed by the feel of the morning sunshine on her dry skin. She smiled at the thought. Her clothes were clean, her tennis shoes were clean, and she was out on this beautiful day. She crossed the street, studying the town as she did. It was a charming country town with wooden and brick shops she looked forward to exploring. But, at this moment, her gaze locked onto the delightful café with its bright-yellow door that made her think instantly of delicious lemon pie. As she was stepping onto the sidewalk in front of the diner, she heard a familiar sound and turned to see a large truck— Chet's truck—coming up the street.

Chet had said he was coming to town, and as he drew close, she saw it wasn't just him. There were two other cowboy-hatted fellas inside. She waved, and Chet, who had his window down and his elbow resting on the opening, looked out and smiled at her—instant electric sparks shot through her—which she ignored.

Tried to ignore.

He parked in one of the slanted spaces and before he had time to get out, the passenger door flew open and out came a good-looking teenaged cowboy. He looked astonishingly like a young Elvis Presley. He wore his cowboy hat on his wavy black hair, had a crooked grin, and striking ice-blue eyes that sparkled as they locked onto her—all he needed was a pair of blue suede shoes and this young man would have all the young ladies *all shook up!*

She almost started singing the songs that always helped brighten her days as she'd struggled through life, as if going back before her time into the fifties and sixties music hits helped her forget her time and the trouble she was lost in. They were songs her mother and father had loved...it was something of them she hadn't forgotten.

Behind him came a taller young man, very muscled and with rusty-brown hair splaying from beneath his straw hat that didn't diminish his eyes. No, those eyes were the color of fading jeans, not as bright as the other teen's eyes but they were brightened when he topped off with a grin that took off like a lightning bolt and *goodness gracious* had her thinking of her other fifties singer's song lyrics she loved and she smiled, blown away by the two young men as they both grinned at her wider—probably because her eyes more than likely widened in shock.

"Wow," she managed. "I mean, good morning," she said, with a chuckle mixed in with her words.

"Yes, it is," Elvis said, his crooked grin hitching more. "We're a couple of fellas from the ranch. I'm Tony—not Elvis Presley if that's what you're thinkin'. I get that a lot."

A big grin busted across her face and she chuckled. "I can see why. Do you sing?" She couldn't help asking.

He shook his head, laughing along with the other young man. "Nope, you know that song he sings about being all shook up—that would be me if I tried to get out there and I'd be looking like a hound dog too."

"Yes, he would," the other cowboy agreed, giving him a nudge with his shoulder.

"You know your songs," she said, enjoying this moment.

"I know who I am, and I know who I *ain't,*" he said grinning. "So, this is my brother, Micah. We heard about your ordeal yesterday and wanted to come check on you, make sure you're okay." He waved his thumb from her to Chet as he spoke. Chet was smiling and she could see laughter in his eyes too at Tony's taking in of her words. "See, instead of standing on stage and singing, I was feeding a baby calf when Chet came by to check on everything last night, and he told me what happened. He was soaked to the bone so I knew something had gone on. Anyway, I had to come meet you and so did Micah. Hope you don't mind."

"Not at all." She was thankful they'd come and had enjoyed his teasing.

"Nice to meet you. Glad you're okay," Micah said, digging his fingertips into his jean pockets as he nodded, those eyes of his concerned.

Her heart swelled. They were caring, and it touched her. Her gaze went from the fellas to Chet as he came up behind them.

"So, how are you?" His gaze was glued to hers.

Tremors sparked through her, and she rocketed her gaze back to the younger cowboys, not needing to look into his deep, navy blue eyes. But her fickle gaze went right back to his. "I'm good," she managed lightly enough. "I'm going inside what I hear is a fantastic breakfast place to try it out." She forced her double-crossing eyes to finally, thankfully, look back to the younger men. "If y'all would like to join me, I'd love to buy you breakfast and hear about the ranch you live on. I cut through that little road because I was interested in the ranch and finding out more about it."

The guys' eyes lit up even brighter with excitement, which gave her more want, more *need* to learn more about the ranch. She'd never, ever have been excited to go back to any of the homes she'd been in, and knew it wasn't the foster parent's fault. Her heart hadn't been in the game…it had been lost. This, their smiles, was inspiring.

"We'd like that," Micah said, his pale jean-toned eyes telling her he really wanted to. "This is the best place to eat. And Miss Jo…well, she's a really sweet lady."

"Yep, sweeter than her delicious pies," Tony added, grinning with that crooked Elvis smile of his.

They were delightful. April's gaze—of its own demand—went to Chet, who grinned, though his navy-blue eyes were now shadowed to near black. "Is that okay with you?"

"Yes, after all we came in to check on you. And you know, meet you in a different way than our meeting yesterday. You doin' okay?"

"I'm great, thanks to you. So, let's get a seat. I've heard a lot about this place."

Tony chuckled. "Wait till you get all the greeting from the cows. This Cow Pattie Café has cows everywhere."

Cow Pattie? Just like Chet had said all the fella's called it. Smiling she started to push the door open when suddenly Chet's arm reached around her and he pushed the door open, standing close as he did so. She looked at him and she felt that crazy tingle again as it traveled all the way to her toes. Instantly, the memory of her irrational kiss the day before swept through her. Yanking her gaze away, she stepped quickly inside and was greeted by cow mooing.

Loud mooing that drew her gaze down to an adorable three-foot, fake black-and-white spotted cow just mooing like it was singing a solo. It was well aged, obviously having been touched so much it was going hairless. One day it would be a bald cow and even more adorable.

The door opening must set it off as a welcome and also an announcement that a new customer had just entered the café. She chuckled, then walked forward so the others could follow her inside. The cow mooed the entire time. Just a few steps inside, she stopped—there were cows everywhere! On the walls were plaques with cow pictures, cow heads, fake but funny faces, boards with cows painted, and all assortment of things. Dressed-up cows, cow clocks, cow puppets—it was hilarious, there were so many. It was definitely a cow-inspired diner. Then she glanced down and saw the black-spotted floor and grinned. Even the buffed-concrete floor was painted like a cow. Large, irregularly shaped brown, almost black spots decorated the floor. It was supposed to be a cow hide.

But... She stared, and Tony's words rang through

her again—*Cow Pattie Café*. Now she got it.

"Welcome," called a short lady as she hurried from behind the counter. "I'm going to guess you're April. And you've got a great group of good-looking men escorting you into my diner."

"Yes that's right." She grinned at the delightful lady whose smile was almost wider than she was tall.

"I'm Miss Jo, the owner of this little place, and so glad to meet you. Chet, so grateful you were there when April needed you." She started down the row and looked around at all the diners who were watching them. April suddenly felt as if she were on a stage as Miss Jo kept talking to everyone. "Now all y'all that might not know this, our Chet rescued this beautiful lady last night. Down there on the low bottom. She wouldn't be with us this morning if he hadn't been there at the right time. So all y'all give them a couple of claps of welcome."

The room, which was full of cowboys and a few women, old and young, all started clapping, welcoming her.

April was floored.

Nothing, *nothing* had ever happened like this in her life.

CHAPTER FIVE

Chet stood back as everyone gave April a Dew Drop welcome. He enjoyed watching it. Home; this was home and he was glad the boys had come with him.

They gave him a little space. They'd been standing together by the barn when he'd gone to pick Tony up and asked if Micah could come along. They were the two oldest boys since Wes and Joseph were now in college. It wouldn't be long until Micah, who was about to turn seventeen, would head to college if he wanted. Tony was sixteen and would be the next to leave for school or whatever he chose to do. He was so proud of them and enjoyed knowing they had become the leaders of the younger boys. And them coming along today was good because as they already had been doing they'd carry on a conversation with April.

He wasn't the best conversationalist, and he was trying to stay distant, so he was glad to have them.

Thankfully, Miss Jo led them to a table by the window at the end of the café. This gave them a little privacy that sitting in the middle of the café wouldn't have done. She understood he didn't want to be the center of attention and knew him rescuing this beautiful woman had probably started some talking.

Don't think about that.

April chose the far side of the booth giving him the benefit of having his back to the rest of diners. Perfect; he wouldn't have to see all the looks they might draw. He waited as she slid into her booth and then he slid into the other side, leaving Tony and Micah to decide who was sitting by him and who was sitting by April. Without hesitation, Tony took the seat beside April. Micah slid in beside Chet and didn't look bothered that he wasn't sitting beside the pretty lady.

"So, tell me, guys—what's good?" April asked as she drew the four menus from the rack on the far edge of the table and passed them out.

"Everything," Tony answered quickly. "Miss Jo and T-bone, the cook, they don't make anything bad. Now, some people don't like everything but that's normal, you know. But most folks taste buds get excited just opening the door and walking inside, and it has nothing to do with little Cow Patty giving them a shout-out like she did when you walked in—and I'm talking about that little play calf, not tiny Miss Jo." He grinned and so did April.

"If you like a bacon and cheese omelet with bell peppers and all kinds of other stuff, then you'll love their omelets," Micah said, and got another smile from April.

"They do great bacon, eggs, and sausage too," Tony added. "And Miss Jo makes all the bread for the toast and all the jams too."

"Yeah, that tops everything but it's all great. The French toast is amazing, and the pancakes too." Micah rubbed his flat belly. "You can't beat them, even with the omelet. That's why I always have a hard time deciding. But, I'll get some bacon on the side for the protein."

She grinned and met Chet's gaze that had stuck to her whether he wanted it to or not. '

"So, I am about to be overwhelmed?" she asked, her words edged with a soft laugh. "Looks like I'm going to have an omelet, a piece of French toast, and a pancake. Do you have any other suggestions?" She chuckled, her smile illuminating.

He couldn't help laughing too. This was a great

morning…he was really glad the fellas had come with him, or he could be in trouble watching the sparkling woman, different from the shaken-up pretty lady who had emerged from the river yesterday. This one was something that reached inside him and…what?

Wish for more.

* * *

Filled with laughter, April watched the two young men and Chet. His eyes locked onto hers and held for the first time since arriving. Her heart, the crazy thing, pounded as if she were playing the drums.

"Well, it's all great. The woman knows how to hire help. The waitress you'll meet soon, is a bit of entertainment, and T-bone is, like the boy implied, one heck of a great cook. Everything he cooks is delicious. And yes, Miss Jo makes all of her own bread and her homemade grape and strawberry jellies." He hitched his dark brows up as he spoke. "But, the prickly pear jelly she orders in, and it's my all-time favorite."

"Yeah, it's great," Tony agreed. "She gets it from a family-owned business in a little town called Mule Hollow, Texas. The woman, Rose—I think that's her name—and her son started making the jelly after they'd had a rough life, like us, and got away and needed to start over. They did it by making prickly pear jelly. Ain't that cool?"

His words sent her heart drumming. "It's wonderful," she said, enveloped in the story.

"They're doing great with the business and the jelly is good," Micah said. "All Miss Jo's is too but I like the story of the prickly pear jelly. I'm glad the lady kept her son, didn't give him up and was able to start over in a new life with him beside her."

April's heart cinched tight at those words, recognizing that Micah related. It was a story so easily taken for granted in the brightness of the ending but all of them sitting at the table knew that not all life had those wonderful starting moments. Micah caught the simple fact that the boy and his mother started a company together. The boy hadn't been given up for adoption, or taken away from her, or lost her because she'd died or been killed... Her heart thundered as she focused on the goodness of the story.

"That's wonderful and such a very encouraging story. I can't wait to taste the jelly now." She smiled gently at Micah, then met Chet's gaze. He gave a slight nod, as if getting that he understood what she'd just seen.

"Miss Jo agrees and is the one who tells the story about the prickly jam for all to know there is a new start in many ways, even ugly, sticker-covered prickly pears," Chet said, his words sincere. "She tells it because the story thrills her. It sends a message of hope and new beginnings. See, we all live on the foster ranch, but Rose and her son were in a shelter, having run from abuse. They'd made it to the tiny town of Mule Hollow and worked hard to make a new start on a farm overrun with cactus. It's a great story. That boy is a young man now, and I'd bet he's happy. Like me and these two, and all the boys at Sunrise Ranch." She saw the depth of serious enragement in his gaze as it took in Tony and Micah. "Your life can start out bad, but if you're determined enough, you can make it good. And from what I understand, that boy had been through a lot, but he and his mom were determined to make their life good. And they did."

His gaze had melted, his words digging deep into her, and now his gaze flickered between both boys. "So what do you say, fellas—are we making our lives good?"

She was so startled, gripped by Chet's words. It was as if he was purposefully showing these two guys sitting beside him that their lives could be happy—not just now but forever—using the kid from another town. And yes, she had heard of Mule Hollow and the cactus jelly, but this made it personal as she watched Micah and Tony. They were listening, and her heart ached with a stunning gratitude for Chet.

Not only had he saved her, but he was making sure he helped these boys realize that just because they'd started out with a bad family situation that their life now was going to be good, and in their hands to make what they chose.

What *they* chose.

Her thoughts whirled with Chet's words basically saying that after a certain age your life was the choice you made. No one else controlled you.

No one.

"Yep, we like that jelly and what it represents," Tony said. "And one day, I hope I meet that kid—man. I think he's older than me. But I think he was around my age when that was going on in his life. He made good from it, for everyone to enjoy. What do you say, Micah—me and you are going to be good, aren't we? We're going to follow after that kid and also Joseph and Wes." He hitched a brow at her. "They just graduated at the end of the year and became college boys. We like when they get to come home and see us, but they're doing great. Micah will get to go before me but we talk about it a lot. We're going to lead the way, like they did.

They came in from a bad past and like Chet here, they led the way for us. And we're going to do the same."

"We take it real serious," Micah added, his gaze agreeing with his words as he looked at April. "I haven't been here anywhere near as long as Chet or even Tony. I only got here a little before Jake, our other brother about our age, but I deal with stuff pretty good. And if something comes in and hits me hard in the memories that tend to haunt us all, I have a lot of help to get me through it."

Her thoughts rolled, knowing she hadn't had that.

Was *this* what Mabel had realized in reading her books? Was this what had signaled Mabel to send the letter?

* * *

"Well hello again," Edwina said, breaking in when she came up to the table.

Chet realized she was looking straight at April as she said "again." *When had they met?*

"So how did you like that chicken pot pie I brought you last night?"

Of course that was how they'd met. He should have figured that out but his head was spinning from the conversation he'd been able to have with the boys just now and then by the startled expression in April's eyes. Now, he watched the wide smile that spread across her face and was glad to see it and not what he'd just glimpsed.

"You were not kidding," April said. "It was unbelievable. It was so good. And like you said, I will have to go back there and tell T-bone what an excellent job he did."

Edwina grinned big. "I'm not wrong about much, and I knew you'd love it. Now, how are you handsome fellas doin'?" She stuffed her hand that held her pen onto her hip, and patted the small order tablet on her other hip as her gaze took them all in. "Y'all know that breakfast is going to end in about thirty minutes, so I'm here to grab your orders and get it back there before ole T-bone starts letting lunch take over. Y'all must have been sleeping late this morning." She hitched a brow high.

Chet laughed, and the boys did too.

Tony patted the table with his hand, grinning up at her. "Miss Edwina, we had things we had to do at the ranch. *I* rescued a newborn calf last night in the storm, and we had to feed him this morning. *Chet* rescued this pretty lady sitting beside me last night, too, and *we* have to feed her now." He chuckled, and his words made them all laugh.

"That's all good stuff," Edwina said, smiling widely.

"Yes, it is," April said, giving Edwina a smile before she looked at Tony. "You rescued a baby calf?"

"Yes, ma'am, I did. He's doing good this morning. I had to feed him again, and Micah is going to help me take care of him because sometimes we have other things we need to do, so we're going to share responsibility for him."

"Yep, we got our hours figured out this morning," Micah added.

"I think that's wonderful," April said.

"I do too," Edwina said. "Do y'all think I need to come check on him and make sure you fellas are doing a good job?" Her expression was serious, but it was just her way, and Chet knew the boys knew it too.

"No, ma'am," Micah said. "We've got it. And if we see we need more help, we're going to pull Jake in. He's there and our age too and will help. We'll take care of it. Plus, you know all those little fellas are going to want to help too. Believe me, that calf is probably going to get treated a *whole* lot better than I was—well, how most of us were treated when we were kids. Those little fellas are going to treat him like he's a big puppy and give him a lot of love."

Chet didn't miss the remark Micah made about

himself. But the young man just kept going like he hadn't meant to say "treated better than I was." But the words slammed through Chet, and his gaze locked onto April's. She'd caught the words too. He knew what Tony had gone through and how good he was doing but Micah—

"I think you are an outstanding group of boys—yes, I do," Edwina said. "I'm glad I don't have to come out there and straighten any of you out because you two help. And have a lot of good fellas like this here Chet to help." Edwina's eyes landed on him, and he was pretty sure she'd caught Micah's hint of his bad past too. "This one is a good fella to teach you or to talk to if you need to talk. I was already working here at the diner when the ranch opened its amazing doors for all you great fellas. This one came in with Morgan, Rowdy, and Tucker, and they all had to get through stuff of their own too. I did it all myself—but I can honestly tell you I didn't have the amazing support of that wonderful group of people out there on the ranch. Still, I'm not sure I'd want to take care of a bunch of cows but after watching all the boys who've come through here it's obvious y'all all love it." She pulled her hand holding the pad up and positioned the pen on the pad. "So, now that I've yacked my head off, y'all do a little yacking back at me and tell me what you want to eat."

Chet pondered what Micah said as everyone placed their orders. He'd planned to pay but April told Edwina that she was paying through the inn for now, until her credit cards arrived. And then she told the boys she was ordering all the food they'd suggested she try. Then she'd looked straight at Micah and told him today he was getting pancakes, French toast, and bacon…and an omelet, too. It was her treat. He laughed inside and gave a grin as the guys went for the offer and made her smile grow even bigger.

He ordered his regular bacon, fried eggs, and toast to go with that amazing prickly pear jelly. But the whole time, his mind was on Micah's words. *Was he still struggling?* Chet was going to have to make sure he was okay. He didn't want Micah growing up and hiding it—well, Chet was hiding his pain but that was him. This was Micah trying to hide his pain and what if he couldn't handle it?

Chet knew all too well that it wasn't easy. He was going to have to look into Micah's background papers. He was pretty sure Micah's parents had divorced and left him behind, not died like his own. If Micah knew who they were, he wasn't interested anymore in finding them. There were some similarities to his own background—if his parents hadn't died in the river incident—from what he heard that night in the back seat. That part haunted him. He knew that if they'd made it through that night, he would have been thrown out, or with one or the other, probably his dad. But he would never know because they'd both died. And that was what hurt Chet the most—not knowing if he'd have been wanted after their breakup or tossed aside.

He'd always told himself his dad would have taken him, because he thought his mom was the one who was in love with someone else… He pushed his past aside, this wasn't about him but about Micah. The almost seventeen-year-old who would be at the ranch only another year before he headed off to college, if he decided to go—that was up to each young man.

Chet had to make sure to help him if he needed it.

"It sounds like we're going to eat some really good food," April said, thankfully turning the topic to food. "Edwina has a sense of humor, I think."

Both the boys grinned. He did too, in relief.

Tony tapped the table with his fingers. "Miss Edwina will tell it like it is. But she cares for us, and I have to say, if there was ever a mishap and one of us was in town in the middle of something gone wrong, she'd step in. And I can tell you, from what I get from the drift of her tales of her three bad husbands she dealt with, she could take care of whatever was going down. From what we get, she had a bad habit of marrying the wrong men. So, I'm just going to tell you, Miss April, when you get married, make sure he's a good man and the right guy. Because Miss Edwina will tell you she will never do that again. *But*," he looked at Chet, "she *does* get her eyes fixed on certain fellas, and right now it's Chet."

Chet's brows met unintentionally at Micah's words. "What? No. That's ridiculous. Edwina and me— no, she doesn't have a crush on me."

He caught April watching, and she had a look of study on her face. As if her brain was working on something and her mouth wasn't. He'd seen that look before—she was thinking hard.

"Well, I kinda agree with Tony," Micah said. "We come in here sometimes and watch while we eat and she takes care of business. If some fella is not acting right, she'll walk over to his table, stick that hand on her hip and tear into him or them—it don't matter—she'll take on a whole table, telling them what they need to do— shut up or get out." He grinned; it quickly turned into a laugh. "They don't even get to finish the meal if they don't straighten up." His face lit up, it was so humorous to him. "Thing is, the food is great, so good, that they always end up straightening up. And we think some of them do it just to see her get after them."

Tony nodded in agreement and then broke in, "It's

another draw to Dew Drop—the Cow Pattie Café, as we all call it for fun, it's good food and entertainment at the same time."

April chuckled. "I'm getting that. I love it. I'm quite entertained by everyone and so far, I'm highly impressed with my visit. I like it a lot and so glad y'all are having breakfast with me."

"Well, we are too," the boys both said together, as if knowing the words coming out of the other's mouths.

Chet smiled at that. "Yes, we're glad you're enjoying it here. And don't believe everything they said. Edwina is one smart woman, and I am not on her target list. Now, here comes breakfast, so let's drop that subject and enjoy this gigantic meal."

"I think you have the perfect idea," April said, beaming bright and happy.

And Chet felt her smile all the way through his body.

CHAPTER SIX

Chet changed the subject as they ate, taking it to her interest in the ranch. And so their conversation had gone there easily. By the time they finished an absolutely amazing, partly not-eaten-too-huge-of-a breakfast, she climbed into the truck with all three of them so she could go see the calf.

Yes, the two boys got in the back seat, and Chet held her hand as he helped her climb up into the truck. The now-dry seat did not distract her from the feel of his hand around hers, and she had to concentrate on being glad the seat was dry and not dripping wet from her time in it last night. Not a wet seat was much better to think about than how firm, secure, and dependable his hand felt on hers.

She couldn't completely ignore the wonderful

feeling of his touch because someone in her book could feel this when the hero of the book touched her. Yes, experience for a book…that was the way she would look at it and not let her feelings get any more personal.

She watched the beautiful day passing as they headed to the ranch. Excitement filled her. She could not wait to arrive. Oh, what a wild trip this had begun as, but now, the second day and not even lunchtime, and she was going to the ranch. The ranch that had inspired her to plan this trip, to see it, and now, to see what would inspire her work.

That was one thing she had learned in her life as a writer: she would contemplate things, and get ideas in her head, and then things would happen that would inspire moments in the books. That was happening right now. She'd already hoped this would be an inspiration. Mabel had brought her here with her letter, and she'd not yet had a long conversation with Mabel. The amazing woman did not know April was B.P. Joel, the writer Mabel had written to—and she would never know it. But not talking about it with her didn't mean that April couldn't explore the other side of foster care. The wonderful side that Mabel said existed through the example of Sunrise Ranch.

It was something she had missed out on, but she could see it just from breakfast with the almost adult—

young men—who would object to the adjective she'd secretly attached to them: adorable. They were strong, smiling men, and yes, she found them adorable.

She prayed one day they'd find a woman who would bring more light into their lives... That thought came out of nowhere and shocked her. She truly did wish that for them though. These wonderful young men who had hopefully happy lives ahead of them, with love and support they got from the people at the ranch and town.

And from Chet, it was in his eyes and the way he spoke with them.

It was a compliment, but she'd never tell them what she thought about them. They looked up to Chet, who was one of them, and when they looked at him, their eyes were full of respect...love. Brotherly love, as if they'd come from the same wonderful mother. And she wanted to meet the woman who inspired that. Yes, they respected the men but somewhere there was a woman. The grandmother she wanted to meet...yearned to meet.

"Are you sure you want to do this?" Chet asked, breaking into her thoughts.

They'd driven down the road, and the boys were talking to each other about it being time to feed the calf.

She focused. "Yes, everything is fine, as long as you have time for this."

"He has time. We all have time. It's time to feed the calf, and you get to do it," Tony said, his Elvis grin meeting her gaze as she looked back at him. "How does that sound?"

"I think it's wonderful. I had no idea I was going to get to feed a baby calf. Never done that before in my life. But I like new experiences, and this will be a good one!"

"So you like experiences, but you don't do a lot, you say. Why…" Tony asked and as usual, Micah was silent.

But she glanced at him, and he was obviously interested in her answer.

"What do you do?" Tony finished, exactly the question she thought he was heading for.

Her mind roared, and as usual she said what she normally said. "I research different things and write about them. That sort of thing."

"You're a writer?" Chet asked.

"Yes, I write about…experiences. I travel all over the country, never staying in one place long. That's just my life. I move around a lot."

"That's real interesting," Micah said before Chet could comment. He leaned forward slightly. "I'm not sure what I'm going to do with my life, but writing articles…sounds interesting. I'm not great in English,

71

but I may have to up my game and pay more attention. Of course, Miss Jolie, our teacher, would be real happy about that. Anyway, you kinda got me to thinking."

From the corner of her eyes, she noticed that Chet, when she glanced his way, had a shocked expression on his face. And Tony had one too, as she saw it while focusing directly on Micah. "I think that's a great idea. You don't have to be great at English, like top of the line, as long as you have an outstanding editor. You just have to know what you want to say with your words, the feel of it, and how you want it to come out on the page. How you want it to touch someone. Most people have a voice inside them that comes out in their work. A voice, a way your readers will enjoy it and know it's you. Your voice is your most important element—it sets you apart."

Micah grinned; she did too.

She'd enjoyed telling him how to do it. She didn't want to tell him what she really wrote—didn't want to tell anyone that. But she had to encourage him, and the spark in his eyes told her she was doing right. If she could help someone, especially someone who had been through similar situations as her, to see writing as a wonderful way of expression, then she would do that. She'd needed a way out of the pain, of the troubles that filled her in her dark closet, hiding from all the lies she'd lived with and watched die. Growing up had been so, so very hard and writing had saved her.

And she suddenly wanted with all of her heart to help someone else find their release. Micah's eyes glowed as his thoughts took everything in. She loved it.

Tony pushed him in the arm and grinned. "Well, boy, I don't know what to think about that. If you write something, I sure want to read it. Are you thinkin' you're going to write travel stories or them romances that a lot of girls read?" He chuckled and April bit back a smile. "Or are you going to write mysteries, or hey, maybe aliens or things like that?"

She was about to burst out laughing as Tony dug in deep with genuine curiosity in his words and eyes, so she held back. In her side gaze, she caught Chet's lips tremble upward as he watched the road. Then she looked directly at Micah and his startled look as he stared at Tony.

"Whoa, boy. I just said I was thinkin' about it. I don't have any idea what I'm thinkin'. I'm just curious. Her talkin' about it spurred something I never thought about before. But you know how sometimes you'll feel a spark inside you? Well, that's kinda what I felt. But I have absolutely no idea what I would write. *Or* if I would write. It was just a thought." He looked so serious as he shot his brother a "get my drift" glare that told

April he was totally startled by Tony's question and reaction.

Tony continued to grin, not taking the hint. "Despite all that, Micah, you thought it. I think it's kinda cool. Me, I would never think about writing. I'm gonna be right here on this ranch, workin' with cattle and workin' with boys who have been through what I have been through. I'm going to copy that man in the front seat. That's what my goal is, ya know? You could write about it. Yeah, that'd be good."

Her heart throbbed at what the kid was saying. She glanced at Chet and saw the smile as he slowed the truck then glanced toward her, emotion in his gaze as he then looked over his shoulder at the young men, sincerity in his eyes.

"Micah, you will do whatever you set your mind to—you have that in you. Tony, we talked some about you staying here, and I'm glad that your heart is where it is, so we'll see where it goes. But neither one of you needs to close the door to other things. Life will show you the way. *God* will if you let Him…in His own timing."

And then he pressed the gas and focused on the road.

She, in that moment, couldn't tear her gaze off him. There was feeling and emotion in his words, but something wasn't quite right. She felt it.

Her head, the creative side, sometimes went into a place while everything else was in another place, and right now she was in a truck full of talking guys in the back seat and one quiet in the driver's seat. And that one had her intrigued and her thoughts churned. That creative spot that was always working on the sidelines as she lived each moment was now working overtime. She never knew what it was going to come up with, but had learned when the time was right, everything would come together and the story revealed. Just as her life had no plot, she was not what was called a plotter in her story telling, no, she was a pantser, her books came as she went, she learned the story as her readers did, one page at a time.

But right now, staring at Chet she knew this had nothing to do with him; her thoughts were reeling over the fact that this conversation was inspiring her brain toward a character and what he or she might end up going through in her coming story.

Emotions were emotions, and they affected people in different ways. But in a lot of ways, they were similar, depending on how deep an emotion it was. She knew that the anger and despair she felt at her parents for hiding her past from her and then only learning she'd been living a lie—learning that while *watching* the man *kill* them—all emotions she tried not to think about suddenly sprung forward—she tried shoving them away. She didn't need them right now. She didn't but...

She wrote suspense, and there were hard moments. She had every kind of emotion available to bring to life in the instances she needed it. But right now...

Right now as she stared at the man beside her, she was completely shocked that she wanted to know what deep thoughts he was thinking and what drove those thoughts.

"Okay, there it is," Tony blurted out. "Our ranch has many entrances." He leaned forward between her and Chet, his elbows on both front seats. "They are made of metal poles and the metal sign has Sunrise Ranch cut into it. See there." He pointed to the sign. "We've got a load of entrances on this ranch. There's something like ten thousand acres here. That's not big like some of them out on the way to Corpus Christi, like that McIntyre Ranch we buy cattle from. That ranch is about a *hundred thousand* acres or something crazy like that. Been thinking maybe I could get a job out there if my dream here doesn't work out. There's some ranches out there bigger than McIntire's—you know, the King Ranch. But, in Texas, ten thousand acres is big, and we're really proud of it. Plus, it has that crazy black stuff on it and that made it possible for sweet Mrs. Lydia's dream of all of us kids calling this home possible." He grinned, his eyes dancing.

She rolled his words over in her head and gave up. "I love that, but okay, I missed something. Crazy black stuff—what is that?"

Everybody in the truck busted out laughing, even Chet, as his cute grin danced through her. She yanked her eyes off him and back to Micah, who was now leaning against Tony as they laughed hard at her probably funny expression.

"Go on. Tell her," Micah said, pushing Tony with a playful fist.

Tony cocked his head, his eyes dancing. "*Oil.* Bubbling crude as Mr. Chili and Mr. Drewbaker like to say. This ranch struck oil a long time ago. And that's what's enabled them—not the cattle and the horses, which are wonderful and give us a great way of learning about life—no, it's the oil that gave them the ability to bring sweet Mrs. Lydia's dream to life. You'll see the pumps scattered out over the land. There is one near the entrance we're going in."

"Yes," Micah said. "If it hadn't been raining so hard last night when you came through on that road where Chet had to save you, you'd have seen a bunch of them scattered over that low land."

"Yep," Tony added. "Pumping black stuff. Good

old oil—exactly what our dreams are made of."

She chuckled; they were so cute and so serious. "Well then, I'm grateful the oil came in because of you guys, oh my goodness, this has been a great morning. And…" She paused as it hit her even more the message Mabel had written in that letter to B.P. Joel. Mabel had felt that what had happened to B.P. Joel had *not* happened to *these* boys. They might have gone through hard times but they had this ranch and obviously these McDermott men and their mother and father and grandmother. And the townsfolk. But the sweet woman whose dream this was had made one thing certain, these boys found real life here. And April knew now she wasn't leaving this town until she figured out about this wonderful place that worked this magic in these boys' lives.

The simple iron gate with a bar across two tall poles and a metal plaque hanging down with the words "Sunrise Ranch" cut into it was the entrance into a life-changing place, and she was going to find out how it worked.

CHAPTER SEVEN

Chet drove onto the ranch and let the boys do all the talking, considering they enjoyed it and obviously April enjoyed it, too. He was aware something about them telling her about the oil had hit her in some way— a good way, he was pretty sure. They were all grateful for the oil. It was a gift from God in the hands of the right people: a woman with an amazing dream, and a family who loved Lydia McDermott enough to make it come true even after losing her.

She'd had the vision and so here they sat, living a life in sunlight rather than darkness.

And now, April was learning the history and seeing where the dream began. When she saw Nana's house, a large two-story home with a welcoming front porch, she gave him a sweet sigh. He liked the sound of it.

"That's where Nana lives," Micah said, beating Tony to it. "You've got to meet her. She's amazing. And her daughter-in-law is the one who had the dream of our foster home being here. And Nana and her son Randolph, they made it come true. And her grandsons— Chet here, too—are our older brothers. They made all her dreams and ours come true. Her dream has and is going to change a lot of lives. And I'll always be grateful."

"Me too," Tony said. "It doesn't all happen at one time. You know, when you've been through a lot and then your life changes…mine didn't at first…" Tony's words softened. "I'm the man I am now after going through some stuff, bad stuff, and my body shows it under these clothes. But, you're going to meet the pretty little Lucy, she's a tiny lady but a great woman. She's married to Rowdy. He helped her overcome some things she went through." He sighed, a gravelly sound, as if his voice faltered with emotion.

Chet knew why. Tony, handsome Tony's poor body was so scarred from the torture put on him from his dad that he was, as far as Chet thought, a walking miracle. God had saved that kid for a reason, and he knew it.

Tony took a deep breath. "Lucy went through a lot but what she went through helped me. I was trying to help her overcome what she'd gone through but doing that helped me move forward and I've been getting stronger ever since she and I talked. We helped each other. And while that was happening, she and Rowdy fell in love." He grinned, as if he hadn't just exposed a deep scar in his life. "Watching people fall in love is pretty cool. It makes me see there is more in life. We watched it with Jolie and Mr. Morgan—" He grinned. "He's our brother but also our ranch leader with his dad, and sometimes the *Mr.* sneaks in on talking about him, even though you're not supposed to call your brother *Mr.* Morgan's a great man to look up to—they all are..." He paused as Chet's chuckle sounded. "Now, Chet, don't go getting all hysterical up there. You know what I'm talking about."

Chet grinned. "Yes, I do. Morgan is our leader and our brother." He looked at April as he pulled the truck to a halt in front of the big red barn.

"Yep," Tony added. "Morgan is the one who took hold of the running of his mom's dream along with his dad. Rowdy is the brother who's a cowboy all the way and learned that love comes from what's inside, not outside. That's important," Tony paused, his hand pinching his shirt.

"That's true," Chet offered, knowing Tony was thinking about his scars beneath that shirt.

"Anyway," Tony continued, clearly taking control over where his mind had gone. "This place is awesome and I could talk all day, but right now let's go see a calf."

"Yeah, sounds good," Micah said and they climbed out of the truck.

Chet looked at April. "He can get to talking and it's hard to keep up. He's been through a lot but he's right— let's go see a calf."

"Okay," she said, but hesitated before reaching for the door handle. "Chet, thanks for bringing them for breakfast so I could meet them."

"Thanks for being so good to them." He smiled and then got out of the truck and rounded the front but before he could get to her door, she was already out and heading toward the barn. They walked inside, and he stood back as the fellas rushed forward to lead the way for April. And he didn't blame them; they really liked her. And she seemed very good for them to be around.

His interest in her—not his attraction—had grown after what she'd said to Micah about writing. In the truck, Chet had glanced in the mirror and saw the absorption of her words shining in Micah's eyes. He wondered whether something would come of that. But also, there was Tony; the kid was probably on the right track. He'd been through so much, and he wanted to give back. In many ways, it was like Chet; so he didn't say anything else. He would just have to watch and be there. Right now, he was watching this beautiful gal who had stepped from his side, and he'd caught the grin on her face as she moved toward the guys waving her forward to see the calf.

"Aww, so sweet," she cooed, and he liked the sound.

He told his mind to get right. People made sounds like that all the time. It was a common female attribute, oohing and awing over kids, food, and all kinds of things. But for some reason, when it slipped from her lips and the way she immediately knelt and gently reached her palm through the metal railing of the stall gate to the small calf, it was sweet. The calf thought so too. The soft sound of her voice urged it to step forward, and it did, then instantly began licking her palm. April smiled and didn't flinch or pull away.

He moved to stand beside her so he could see her expressions as she looked down at the calf, which he acted like he was watching. He didn't want the boys seeing him looking at her and getting any ideas. That was the last thing he needed. He knew that all the boys had gotten ideas about Morgan, Rowdy, and Tucker, and in their own sneaky ways had helped the three brothers get things right with the women they were falling in love with at the time. These fellas helped them find the ones they loved. The ones they wanted to marry.

There was the difference. He didn't want to fall in love with anyone.

He didn't want to get married—he wanted to avoid it.

"You are a beautiful, completely adorable baby," April cooed as her hand gently rubbed the calf's forehead. The calf innocently put its back up against the fence and dug his head into her palm to get more of her tenderness on his forehead. And as Chet suspected, he wanted his back rubbed too, thus rubbing against the railing. And April didn't miss a beat. She instantly placed her free hand through the fence and began to stroke the calf's back while she continued to pet him between his big brown eyes that were hooked on her.

Chet's were, too, as her soothing words continued.

"That's a *good* baby. And I'm thinking these boys are taking great care of you. But I bet you're ready for your next meal, sweet girl." She looked at awestruck Tony and Micah and smiled.

Chet almost smiled but bit his lip to stop it though the boys were watching her and wouldn't have noticed even if he'd grinned from ear to ear. They watched her as if they were the ones getting rubbed on the head and getting their back massaged. Oh boy, this little gal had big admirers and well…he didn't blame them. They were teens and were interested in girls; at church, they had girls their age and they hung out together before and after service. And sometimes when there were church get-togethers, all the girls would be there, and they'd huddle up and visit, sitting on the logs that surrounded a campfire. He remembered those days, although he wasn't one of the ones out there visiting with the girls. No, he'd watch from his position, leaning against a tree several yards away. Sometimes one of his brothers, Morgan usually, would come over and visit because at that time they were both adjusting to hard times.

April was too old for them, but what she was doing, and the sweetness coming from her, was a good thing. If they were going to fall in love one day, he wanted it to go right. The last thing these boys needed was to marry the wrong woman. Go through ordeals that led to divorce. He hated it for so many people who went through that but his wish—no, his prayer—was that these boys could find the love of their life their first go-round. And that things would be good for them for the rest of their lives. Their normal, sweet rewarding lives.

When they looked up at him, he smiled because he wanted to encourage them.

And he sure hoped that was what he did, encourage them, not give them the idea that he was thinking the same thing they were: how beautiful this woman was and what a wonderful catch she would be for some lucky man.

* * *

April loved this. As she petted the sweet calf, who clearly wanted and needed loving, her heart broke because the calf didn't have her mama to be loving on it, licking on its forehead, tenderly feeding it and showing it how life would be. Just like she'd seen cows do from a distance. No, this calf had an iron fence around it and some young men—no, cowboys—they deserved that title. Like the guy standing beside her shoulder looking down, who she was making sure she didn't look up at.

She didn't want to send any wrong messages. Her heart pounded so hard right now with the want of a baby—something she never let herself think about. So she certainly wasn't going to let herself look up at this good-looking man who had caught her attention. She didn't need to take a chance of there being any glimmer in her eyes that said *I am attracted to you.* No, she kept her attention on the calf and the boys and pushed *that* thought away.

"So, guys, this is adorable, and she looks like she's ready to eat. So I'll just stay here and let y'all get her food while I give her a little mama love. How does that sound?"

The guys were staring at her with wide eyes and it was, well, a compliment. She saw attraction in a lot of men's eyes when she walked in places, and she wasn't looking for that but she recognized it. *Or was this a case of missing having a mother give them attention like she was by petting this sweet little calf like it was hers and she loved it?* Her heart cinched tight. Her voice rattled as unshed tears rolled down the back of her throat and curled in her stomach. Oh, how she wished these boys had had that. And oh, how glad she was that they'd found this wonderful place.

As the guys walked away to get the bottle prepared farther down the alley, she looked up. She couldn't help it; she kept petting the calf but looked up at Chet, and he was looking at her. His eyes had that sparkle in them, not of adoration or attraction. She could tell that he, like her, fought off that kind of thing. *So what was it?*

"You are a good lady."

His quiet words, spoken in that low voice so the boys wouldn't hear, touched her. "Thank you. It's not hard to be around the kids—these men…at least soon to be. Oh, Chet, I'm praying that the right young woman will come along for each of them." Her words had struck the center of the target board as his eyes suddenly brightened with a shimmer of emotion that made his eyes sparkle. Instantly, he looked away; she did not.

Seconds later, he looked back. "Yeah, it's something I hope they find. Something I'm not going to lead them in because I'm not going there myself. But my brothers—Morgan, Rowdy, and Tucker and how happy they are—are perfect. They can lead them because I can tell in the way they look at you that there's a combination of needs in that look. Both sweet mom, like you're being to that calf, and sweet wife one day."

His words struck like an arrow in her heart. A good arrow if there really was such a thing, like one of those hearts with an arrow through it was supposed to be a good thing. Not for her. Still, she smiled and told herself to get hold of herself.

* * *

He watched her. Every muscle around his heart was tightening, so he couldn't speak.

She did. "Well, I'm not on the market, I don't plan to ever marry. Just not on my agenda. But I'm glad that I can hopefully be an example of a nice young woman who they can fall in love with one day. I don't know if you're thinking what I'm thinking, but it would be wonderful after what they've been through if they could find the right woman and always have her beside him."

He found his voice at those words. "We are on the same wavelength on that one. Yeah, I want them to have a forever love. I think that's what has always haunted me about my parents. My last night with them…" He paused as he glanced to see whether they were still mixing up the formula. They were. Then his eyes met hers again. "I was in the back seat and I'd noticed some off moments between them, but I was young and I didn't recognize things. But they suddenly started talking vehemently about divorce and about the affair my mom was having…with no acknowledgment that I was sitting in the back seat. I learned about everything during a horrible, horrible rainstorm like you were in last night. Those were the last words I ever heard them speak, and my life changed after that. I guess my want to ever step out like Morgan, Rowdy and Tucker did died that night too. Their mom and dad deeply loved each other and that's what they saw and still do with how Randolph carries out her dream. Her dream helped me and I want to carry it on too. I want all these boys to know they can have full lives. And, I…well, I don't worry about myself. I'm comfortable here, and I love this ranch and the people and the idea of helping each of them find their way. Everyone is looking for a calling, and I think you must have found it in writing your articles, the stories that you write. The stories—the articles, I'd like to read. Well, I found my spot here. When the boys look at me and tell me I'm doing the right thing, then I'm satisfied."

Tears swelled in her eyes and he wanted to put his arms around her, lift her up and just hug her, feel her closeness, feel her head resting against his heart. It was something he had never been drawn to before.

Thankfully, the boys came back right then and interrupted the wrong emotions that were cratering through him. She tore her eyes from him—blinked, he was sure—and they welcomed the guys back.

He needed a break but he looked at the guys, not worried they'd see anything he didn't want them to see in his eyes, because they only had eyes for April.

Welcome to the club.

CHAPTER EIGHT

April instantly blinked the tears away, hoping they would think that it was from watching this sweet calf. And if they said anything, that's what she'd say.

The boys took in her eyes, smiled, and told her to follow them through the gate. They were going in.

"Thank goodness…this is a great experience." The words *thank goodness* were supposed to have been in her brain but had blasted out verbally from the position of Chet standing so close to her. The *thank goodness* was of being able to move away from him; the last part was to cover her emotion his nearness caused her. Now, she could think about the calf and not the man leaning against the railing. The cowboy she had been wanting to throw her arms around and tell him he was an amazing man. That he deserved a beautiful life with a wonderful woman. Her parents had had that. They just hadn't lived long enough to enjoy their love with her though.

She followed Tony and Micah into the pen, and Chet closed it behind them, staying outside with his arms locked on the top railing as he watched them. She was glad that he stayed there because the last thing she needed was to be close to him or have him showing her how to feed the little animal. Tony handed her the bottle, told her how to hold it, and then Micah squatted down and she did too. Tony did also, grinning—he obviously enjoyed showing her how to do this. It was clear in his gaze.

Micah beamed. "I'll keep the calf in line so she doesn't get excited and knock you down."

"She won't," Tony said. "You're going to do this good. I just know it. Now, hold it out but be ready because she's going to grab it. She does it well, you'll see." He laughed.

The calf had spotted that bottle. Instantly, it reached out and grabbed hold of it with her teeth and yanked. She had a good two-handed grip on the big bottle but as the baby tugged, she lost balance in her crouched position and ended up flopping onto her rear and sitting in the straw on the stalls floor. She chuckled, held on, and watched the calf enjoy the milk.

Then, suddenly, a bunch of loud, happy voices

burst into the barn. One glance and she saw a herd of younger boys racing in their direction.

Tony laughed. "I was wondering when they were going to show up. It's Saturday, no school and no church. Which is where we will be tomorrow. You'll have to come—you'll like it. But I was wondering when they were going to come out and about and see we were here."

"Yeah, we'll introduce you. There's a bunch of good little boys in this group."

She held tight to the bottle but her gaze locked onto the first little boy—big cheeks, brown hair; he was small but racing their way. She thought he was going to throw himself at the gate he was running so hard, but then he put the brakes on and slid to a halt right before he reached Chet. Then, grinning, he made a slow couple of steps to the gate and folded his arms on the top of the middle rail, barely able to cross his elbows on that rail he was so small. Another little boy came behind him and locked his elbows on the same rail and beamed hugely. The others, all looked around eight to eleven, made it to stand behind them. The last few, who were closer to Tony and Micah's age, came slower and stood behind the young boys—they clearly had let the smaller boys reach them first.

"I'm B.J.," the first boy said. "We heard from these

two that you almost died last night—if that was you—but our brother," he looked up at Chet, grinning, "saved you."

"Yes, he did, thank goodness. I'm April."

"He's good at that stuff. I'm Sammy. I just turned eleven, so that's why I'm smaller than Jeb and Caleb so they let me hang onto the rails." The little boy beamed, not looking at all bothered about being small. "It don't matter that I'm small, I'm going to be tough one day, just you wait and see. I'm working on it."

She smiled and almost chuckled but controlled it. "Nice to meet you," she said liking the way his eyes sparkled, she had a feeling even if he didn't grow to be huge, he'd have a big, fun attitude.

"Yep, you will be," Tony said. "You got in that river when you shouldn't have—you were too little, but you've been doing good since then. And your life was spared for some reason, so we're all looking forward to seeing you grow up, little fella."

That was when she knew, and agreed with Tony—maybe being here on this ranch was his calling because his words made little Sammy grin like there was nothing more wonderful to hear.

Beside him, little B.J. chuckled. "Yeah, I like it here too but I ain't gonna do like Sammy and try to ride down crazy rapids and get caught by that river." He looked at her. "*You* did it accidentally but Sammy did it on *purpose* in a kayak last year. He didn't even know how to work a kayak but wanted to try."

She was startled by this and nearly gasped.

"Yep, it was way too big for him," Tony added, meeting her gaze. "But our Jolie went in there and rescued him. So, if you decide you want to go kayaking like this little dude did, let her teach you first. That's what we're doing now, taking lessons from her, not to go down wild rapids but to go downstream or in the lakes and fish."

"That sounds much better," she managed, loving the way they talked about it.

"Calm waters are the way to start," Sammy added. "One day I might go through the rough waters again, but this time only if Jolie thinks I'm good enough. Believe me, I learned my lesson."

"But what she's teaching us is fun," a blond boy said. "I'm Caleb, and I enjoy fishing. But mostly we take care of calves, like you're doing. Do you like it?"

She loved this, and her heart beat with excitement as she looked into the eyes of these boys standing outside the gate. All these interested boys. "I'm loving it. This is a sweet little girl—right, guys?" She looked at Tony as all the boys laughed.

"Yes, ma'am," little B.J. said. "She's a *girl,* and

ain't never gonna be no bull or no steer. She's gonna be a heifer first, then a mama one day. We like cows."

Oh, goodness, she was so glad she'd come here.

It had thrilled the boys to watch her first time to feed a calf. They'd been cute and the older boys had hung back, grinning as they watched.

The calf had just finished, and she was headed to the gate when she saw an older woman enter the barn.

"Hello there," the lady called, her voice pleasant as it flowed through the barn. Everyone turned at the voice to look at the tall, lean, beautiful older woman with a long gray ponytail swinging as she strode down the alley. She wore worn blue jeans and a straw cowboy hat pushed back on her head, exposing her face and a wide welcoming grin. Everything about her, including her red western shirt with flowers splayed across it, was happy and inviting, just like she appeared to be.

April could just see her in a book! Everything about the woman spoke of her spirit as she came to a halt beside the older boys. April glanced around at the boys; their smiles as they looked up at the woman and told her this was the woman, the grandmother, who had helped bring this dream to reality.

"I'm Nana, and I had to come meet you," she practically sang. "I heard a few rumors at breakfast this morning from these cowboys." She waved her hand at the boys in the walkway, and then grinned at Tony and Micah. "Who heard it from you two that y'all went to town to meet the woman our wonderful Chet saved." Everyone laughed as she hitched her brows up at Chet, and then she looked back at April. "I had to come meet you. I'm so very glad you're safe. I'm glad God put Chet in your path."

She stepped forward and the boys parted, the picture vibrant in April's mind as the sweet lady walked up to her and took her hand between both of hers and gently patted the top of her hand. "My girlfriends call me Ruby, short for Ruby Ann McDermott. These are all the boys I claim, and my boys call me Nana so you can call me whatever you want. You'll hear Nana more than Ruby and hardly ever Mrs. McDermott. I'm one of those who doesn't care to be formal, though I did love my Harrison with all my heart and took his name on our wedding day but now I prefer to be on a first name basis."

Nana hadn't let go of April's hand yet, and her engaging smile was etched across her face. Her blue eyes sparkled like glitter, dark blue overpowered by light blue, all mingled together by the sunlight. This was a special woman, and not because of the color of her eyes but the care and love radiating from their depths. "We're so glad you came. How's everything going?"

April glanced around and all the boys and their smiles agreed with her thoughts, they loved their Nana and she understood why. She avoided looking at Chet as she brought her gaze back to Nana. "I'm doing great. And yes, Chet…" She finally let her gaze go to his, and he, too, was grinning. It was completely clear that this was the woman they looked on as their mother. Their new mother, the one who had helped rescue them and raise them in this wonderful spot.

She looked back at Nana. "He came into that water, and he had to struggle a little because the driver's door, the one I was desperately trying to get open from inside with no luck, wouldn't budge. Then he came around to the other side and pulled it open. I was in so much shock, trapped inside as the water rose around me. I couldn't move…then he held his hand out to me, and it was like a gift from God."

What was she saying?

Her words just came out, uncontrolled. "I grabbed it, and he pulled me out, then carried me through that water up the incline until we collapsed on the side of the hill. We were just barely in the water." Why, *oh why*, was she saying so much?

"Wow," Sammy said. "Keep going. Tell us what happened. I remember when Jolie came in and rescued me. Saved me. I'll never forget that."

She glanced around, and everyone watched her with deep interest. "I'm glad you got rescued too. Chet got me up the hill after we both caught our breath." She did not look at Chet because he and only he would know that crazy her had gone and kissed the man. Her insides shivered at the memory.

Move forward.

"Then we moved up that hill to his *humongous* truck." It was time to get some humor into the story. "That is one big truck and to me, who had my troubles because I was driving a very low to the ground, small car—where I shouldn't have been in that kind of weather. Well, it was another gift from God. I knew looking at it that I was not going back in the water." That got her a laugh from all the boys.

"It's a giant," little B.J. declared through his chuckles.

"And exactly what I needed. He had to help me inside and then he brought me to this amazing town, and the Dew Drop Inn, and now I'm getting to meet all of you wonderful young men. A terrible ordeal turned into an awesome experience." Her heart was beating rapidly as she looked into the eyes surrounding her.

"And that was actually why she told me she'd come here," Chet said, his voice gentle as it rang over the quietness as everyone stared at her.

"So," Nana said, drawing out the two letters. "You were coming here, to our ranch?" She patted April's hand that she was still holding and then released it and placed her hands on her hips. She cocked her head to the side, her gray ponytail swinging and that grin fading to one of concentration, clearly interested in what had brought April to the ranch.

This left April with no other alternative than to elaborate. "Yes, I had read about this wonderful place and was drawn to come and check out the ranch and Dew Drop. I read articles about your wonderful home for all these great boys and interviews from some of the now adult men about how much they loved it here and the town. So, I had to come check it out, add to that the article about the reunion Dew Drop holds for them each year and it just sounded unique. So, I decided to come visit. My only mistake was deciding to take that little tiny road that cut through the ranch and on a stormy night. Needless to say, I shouldn't have done that, I was just looking forward to seeing some of those cows I'd read about."

"And then she drove on that little bridge that always goes under water in a heavy rain." Sammy grinned. "It's almost like we need to go down there and put a gate on it so when it rains, people have to turn around. But have we ever had anyone go on it in a storm?"

"No," Chet said. "We never have, but y'all know I always go down and check that area during a storm."

"And we are so glad you do," Nana said. "We are really glad to have you visit and that you got to see a newborn calf. So, now what are you going to do? You know, our get-together is at the end of the month, and you're welcome to come. We always have a wonderful time. How long are you staying?"

"I really don't know. I...just travel, with—honestly, I sometimes stay in places two, three, and once four months. It depends on how my brain is working and how much I like a place. I have a feeling I'll be here roaming around at least until the end of the month and would love to come to the gathering."

All the guys whooped, hooted, or said *Awesome!* Even the big guys joined in; Tony, Micah, and another young man about their age were grinning. She assumed he was the one who was going to help them with the calf. She laughed at their excitement, then looked at Chet and was floored by the look of disturbance she saw there.

She quickly looked away; his eyes had dimmed and his smile had gone to straight lips, as if he were concentrating on something or...worried about something.

Nana reached out and thankfully distracted her.

"I'll tell you what—Miss Jo and Mabel are going to be excited. They love newcomers, and we have a great time getting to know everyone. You'll have to come to the afternoon sit-down and relax time we three share most afternoons at the diner when it's slower. I'm sure Mabel is already thinking the same thing, but I'll make sure she lets you know. Right now, I have to go get lunch ready for all my boys. I just dropped by before I headed that way. Now, if you're hungry, you're welcome to stay."

"Thank you, I'm really tempted but I need to go back. I so enjoyed meeting all you cowboys." She looked around at all the boys and teens.

"We've enjoyed meeting you," Caleb said.

"Sure have," Tony added, then he grinned as if he'd been whopped with a great idea. "We're having a cattle drive next Friday," he said, enthusiasm in his words. "You want to come? You'll have fun." He looked from her to Chet. "She could come along, couldn't she?"

Chet looked stunned then gave a crooked grin. "You can ride with us, if you want."

She was so thrown off by the suggestion that she didn't say anything for a second.

"You'll like it," little B.J. said grinning.

Oh dear, he was adorable. "I'll think about it and let you know."

Whoops erupted and she had to smile as she

watched the enthusiasm in them. They loved to herd cattle and would like her to join the fun. It was very tempting.

The blond who liked to fix things—Caleb she thought was right—grinned. "You know, in town, at the florist shop that's Abe's mom's, when they came here, they went on a cattle drive with us. And after Tucker saved her from the water she married him. So now she's our aunt." At his words everyone was watching her and she wasn't sure what to say. "Anyway, if you want to talk to her about it go into her store, the flower shop. She's really nice."

Feeling really odd suddenly, she was ready to go. It was as if they thought she might have liked the fact that a couple could fall in love on a cattle drive an odd place for that to happen, but were they thinking she might want to find out how to do it? Her thoughts went instantly to Chet…they had met in a very odd way. *No, not going there.*

What was she thinking?

"Okay, guys, I'm going to take April back to town," Chet said, probably because he realized she was speechless. "If any of you boys want to help feed this little calf, the older fellas will let you help. Just show up and they'll give you the chance. Thanks for coming by, Nana, and I'll talk to y'all when I get back." He turned to her and waved his hand for her to go first. "Ladies first."

It was as if he was ready to get out of there too. She told the boys goodbye and thanked them for a great morning, then she strode toward the exit. It was time to go back to normal in a hotel room all by herself. To calm the sudden racing of her heart.

* * *

Chet was in trouble. He'd known it was coming. He'd felt it when all the boys' looked from him to April. He'd felt it in their gazes. These fellas had somehow decided that their job was matchmaking.

Nope. Nope. Nope. They were not going to think that after he showed them that he wasn't a man to be matchmade.

Oh sure, he thought she was beautiful, wonderfully nice, and good with them. But that didn't mean he was going to give up and say "I do." Nope, he wasn't made for that. He wasn't ever going through the pain that a bad marriage could cause.

They reached the truck and he opened her door then took her arm and helped her as she climbed up on the step and into the truck. She didn't look at him and he realized she also felt something was going on. He didn't say anything, his mind whirled as he closed her door, strode around the front then made himself open his door and get inside. He started the engine, and backed out a bit just as all the kids came outside and started waving goodbye. They were all grinning like there was indeed something brewing.

Nana waved also, gave a pretty smile, then headed toward the chow hall where she did all the cooking and absolutely loved it. In that instant, though he'd never been drawn to the kitchen to cook, he suddenly wished he was heading that way with her.

But no, he was driving down the lane with the woman who, so far, in the short, less than twenty-four hours they'd known each other, had put a flaring roadblock in his path. And he didn't know what to do with it. What was he going to do about the wrong idea he was certain the boys all had?

Get her back to town and out of his truck was the first thing. But he made himself not floor the gas pedal. Made himself drive a normal speed down the road, figuring the boys were watching as far as his truck stayed in sight.

"I had a wonderful time," April said, breaking into his runaway thoughts. "The boys are wonderful, not always sure where their thoughts are going but I adored them."

"Yeah, I feel the same way sometimes."

She turned slightly toward him in the seat. "What about my car? Do we know—I mean, I really feel like it might not have survived. I'll be going shopping this afternoon after you get me to town. I was going this morning but I got a great surprise when all of you came and had breakfast with me and then gave me this treat of coming to the ranch. But I know I'm going to need some things to wear. Even if my car is out and drained my clothes might be ruined. Have you heard anything about my car? If it's gone... I can order a new one this afternoon."

Her words struck him; she'd said she could order a new one, a Mercedes, as if it were just a new pair of pants or a dress or a soft drink. "I didn't tell you because I didn't know how upset you'd be, but you sound like you'll be fine. It wasn't there when I got back there to check on it."

"Really?" she gasped.

Her words had caused him to tell her the truth about her car in a less than gentle way. But the gasp and look in her eyes suddenly told him how she'd said the previous words had been a coverup. He was an idiot.

"I'm sorry but it went downstream. And we're now waiting to see who finds it." He'd slowed to a stop as her face grew more shocked.

"You're waiting to see who finds it? You mean it…it was that bad…" She gasped. "I could have been in it." She closed her eyes.

Instantly, he wanted to reach out and pat her shoulder. No, he wanted to caress the tension from her forehead that had appeared as the few seconds passed. "Hey, I got to you," he said, gently.

She opened her eyes and stared at him. They were now stopped near the ranch's exit. "Thank you." Her words were soft, trembling even. "We now know for certain that if you hadn't come along, I'd have been in that car somewhere out there and no one would have even known it until the car turned up." Tears glistened in her eyes. "You saved my life. No one else would have found me."

"No, you'd have made it out." He said the words despite feeling it wasn't true.

"The door wasn't coming open. I was out of my mind in panic and not even thinking about the other door. And I'm not even a panicking type of person, so that tells you how desperate I was. The water was filling up inside, and you…you rescued me. I'll forever be grateful to you for that."

He heard the tears in her words, the emotion wrapping around him in a stranglehold. He'd felt the same way when that man had pulled him from where he was latched onto the scraggly tree in the middle of the river after he and his parents had been swept into a raging flooding river. He'd clung to it all night long, shivering and crying. Desperate for someone to come through that rushing water and pull him to safety.

He was thankful he'd been able to hang on all night, thankful for those scrawny, waving limbs that had helped hold him in place. And now thankful that he'd been able to pay that moment forward—helping someone like he'd been helped.

He liked the feeling. In fact, he didn't want anyone to have to go through the terror he'd been through, the terror he'd seen in April's eyes. But he'd been glad that somehow God had placed it in him to go and help someone else. And for just that moment he'd been able to pull this sweet woman…this beautiful woman…to safety.

"I'll always be thankful God put me in that place to help you. So, believe me when I say I was just there doing His work. He used me, so I have to say that He probably has a reason—that wasn't your time to go away."

He hadn't pushed the gas pedal, so they were still sitting there. Her face was pale and in shock, no tears anymore, and it was as if he could see her mind working. She would do that sometimes, he'd noticed—just disappear into deep thoughts. He decided it was time to get moving, to get back on track. He tore his eyes away from hers and as she turned her head and looked out the passenger window he pressed the gas.

He drove, not saying anything because he knew from that look on her face that she was lost in thought. He didn't want to disturb her. He didn't know exactly whether it was a good thing or whether she was terribly hurting. Or whether she was thinking about what God might want from her after having her survive that horrible ordeal.

He once again said a quick prayer of thanks. He didn't know why God had used him, but he'd been there in the right spot at the right moment to do what he hadn't been able to do as a kid: save his fighting, angry parents.

CHAPTER NINE

They didn't talk on the way in. It was as if he knew she needed time to adjust. Realizing that, yes, she truly had been going to die. Last night, her car still clung to that fence when they'd left. There was an inkling of worry in the back of her mind but she'd been pushing it away. And she'd had the distraction of breakfast, then the calf and all the wonderful boys.

Now this.

Knowing her car hadn't been located meant if Chet hadn't come along...she'd have been trapped inside, dead.

Her thoughts rolled as he drove. She rode silently, looking out her window. *She owed him so much.*

He pulled to a stop in a parking space of the inn and on impulse, she reached over and laid her hand on his shoulder—his muscled, firm shoulder…the strength that had pulled her from the car and carried her to safety. She squeezed, emotion in her touch as she fought to find words. "Thank you," she managed. "I'll always be indebted to you. But right now, I have to go to my room. I have things to think about. Thank you. It was a wonderful morning—and I'm glad to be alive. Again, my past…this isn't my first time to realize, somehow, for some reason I lived."

Thoughts of her sweet mother and strong dad surfaced. They'd witnessed a killing and testified against a powerful man, then had given up everything to start a safe life…a *safe life* for her and them. But, in the end, she'd lived but lost them.

She shook the thoughts away. "I have to go. Thank you."

"Wait, I need your number in case we find the car and I need to call you." She turned back to him. In soft words she gave him her number and he typed it into his phone. "I'm going to send mine to your phone now that I have this so if you need me, call. Serious, call me."

Her gaze lifted to his and her lips curved slightly in acknowledgment. "I'll be fine."

She opened the door and stepped down; then, after closing the door, she rushed to the inn, needing to be alone.

* * *

Chet watched the door of the Dew Drop Inn close behind a clearly disturbed April. He prayed that she would feel better. On the spur of the moment, he backed out of the parking space and instead of driving on, he pulled across the street and parked in front of Suzie McDermott's flower shop.

He didn't hesitate as he climbed from the truck. It was a wonderful small-town florist, everyone said, and as he walked inside for the first time, he saw what they said was true. He'd never needed flowers before but it was pretty, with the yellow-toned walls, and flowers and gifts everywhere. And behind the counter stood Suzie in her bright-blue dress surrounded by the overflowing flowers of her shop.

Behind her, in the back room, standing at what looked like a work table, was Abe. Abe must have heard him come in because the teen looked his way and grinned. "Hey there. You won't believe it, but I'm making a wreath for Mrs. Shasta. Her little dog she loved a lot died and she came in here and asked me— *me*—to make it a wreath to put on its little grave in her backyard. She said she saw me playing with Spot when I was walking one day and it made her smile that I would do that. So, she wanted me to do this, and I couldn't turn her down. I never made one before. Thank goodness Mom showed me what to do."

Chet's throat tightened up. Wow, today was all about people dying, animals dying. Yep, he needed some flowers. He was just happy to come in and see a bunch of the pretty, bright and soft-toned beauties. "Well, you're doing a great job, I'm sure. And she knew that you would."

He looked at Suzie; she was studying him. "You look troubled. Is there anything I can do? You're not here for flowers for someone's death, are you?"

He placed his hands on the counter, kind of gripping it. "No, thank goodness. I'm here...okay, so I'm sure you heard I had a thing last night." *Stop stumbling around.* "I rescued a lady from a flooding river."

"Yes, I did. I went over and grabbed a couple of breakfast orders for me and Abe because I had a lot of work, so we came in early. I heard but, that was early, and I haven't heard anything else. Is everything okay? Did something happen?"

He shook his head. "No. Actually, Tony, Micah, and I came to town this morning to check on her and ended up taking her to late breakfast—or, I should say, she took us, since she insisted on paying for it. Then the guys started talking to her about the calf Tony rescued yesterday and the feeding of it, and she ended up going out to the ranch with us. She enjoyed feeding the calf and then all the boys came and met her. You know how they are—they embraced her with their enthusiasm.

"And Nana met her. She was, as always, real sweet. Everything was good, but on the way out to bring her back to the inn, she asked me about her car. I guess you heard it caught on a line of fence down in the water where the river had risen and was all the way over the bridge, so thank goodness for the fence."

"I heard that. It helped hold her long enough for you to get to her."

"Yes, she would have hit that bridge and been totally submerged…it would have been bad. But thankfully I got there and got her out. I hadn't told her that when I went to check on it this morning, it wasn't there. The fence broke like I feared it would, and the car is gone. I've put the word out that the car is missing, a small two-door, so hopefully it will be recovered. I've alerted everyone that there is no one inside. That's always a relief to know when you're looking for a submerged car. Anyway, I didn't have to tell her all that—it struck her without saying how close she'd come to being…" He couldn't say it, but thankfully Suzie reached out and patted one of his hands.

"I understand."

"I couldn't tell her last night that this was what I thought was going to happen, and I'm glad I didn't. I was afraid it would hit her hard, and it did. She's okay; she didn't talk after I told her. Anyway, I got to thinking, and I don't know if you can send it right now, but you know how you do all these happy flower arrangements? Nothing romantic, please—no roses or flowers that say that in a secret way—like Chili did when he sent Nana those flowers when you first came to town."

She smiled. "And still does sometimes."

He grinned, knowing the old man had a big thing for Nana but she was not letting him too close at the moment. He wasn't sure she ever would because she'd really loved her husband. He knew people fell in love again, but he just wasn't sure about Nana. It did give everyone something to watch and wait for, and he thought there were a few bets going on.

"So anyway, just some bright flowers that will welcome her to town and make her smile. Does that sound okay? And put on there something like *From Chet—hope you're doing better today.* Or something like that. Not sad. *I'm glad I was there to help you.* That sounds okay, right?"

Suzie smiled gently. "It sounds perfect. It was wonderful you were there at that time. And Chet, I know about your parents and you losing them. That had to be hard for you, so I'm glad you were able to be there for someone else."

"Yes, like the man was for me when he pulled me out. The man whose name I never got. But anyway, thanks for doing this. How about if you take it in the morning?"

"I'll work on it today and take it over there early in the morning. Now I hope you have a great day."

"Thanks." He turned, then looked over his shoulder. "Bye, Abe, and good luck with that. I know you're going to make that lady happy."

"I'm aiming for it. I know my mama does a lot, and I'm going to do good by this dog."

Chet was smiling when he walked out the door because of the boy's enthusiasm about helping out the lady who'd lost her dog. He glanced at the inn as he opened the door of his truck; then he climbed in and started the engine. He thought about everything all the way home. Mostly, though, he hoped the flowers would make April smile.

* * *

The day after she learned that her car had gone down the river and disappeared, April woke up and stretched as she looked up at the ceiling and thanked God that she was here and alive. She hadn't gone out after getting back to the inn and her room. She'd called over to the diner and asked whether they could send another special of the day, and sure enough, Edwina had brought it over. When she'd opened the door, Edwina had sauntered into the room, carrying a tray with a metal lid. Because it wasn't raining, there was no bag. No, she'd lifted the lid and there, on a sandstone plate, was a wonderful chicken fried steak, mashed potatoes and gravy, and corn on the cob—fresh corn on the cob, Edwina stated. And then she'd lifted the lid off a small plate, and there was an amazing piece of coconut pie.

"This is a much-loved pie that came from the founder of the boys' home on Sunrise Ranch, Lydia McDermott. There was never a better cook or woman, according to Miss Jo, and if she says that, I believe her. So enjoy." And then she turned; without another word, she headed out the still opened door.

She'd been right—the entire meal was delicious and the pie was heavenly. April had needed something to help her crazy, mixed-up emotions, and something about that pie made her close her eyes and just simply enjoy the sweet taste while her mind wrapped around and cherished that *she* was still alive.

It hit her then that this was her dinner of celebration because she was alive and in this wonderful town.

And her head was full of ideas.

Now, looking up at the ceiling, awake, she sat up. Today, she was determined to get out of bed, have a delightful breakfast across the street early, and then she'd finally go buy herself something else to wear other than the clothes she'd had on during her "episode." Her credit card should arrive this morning and she was glad, she needed something else beside the same clothes she'd worn for two days, and this time they hadn't been washed. She had to go shopping, first thing after breakfast. Then, if there was any place in town she could order a computer, she would do so. Or she'd order it online, because she now had the urge to write so badly that there was no pushing it away.

Thank goodness she still had her phone and could connect to the internet that way. Then, she was ordering a car...cross that out—nope, she was ordering herself an SUV, a big one. If she ever went off a bridge again, she was going to have a lot of windows and plenty of room to swim to each one and a sunroof—yes, a sunroof to climb out of if needed. There was going to be so many escape places in that vehicle that it wasn't going to be funny. She paused as she thought that...then said a prayer for everyone in that situation. She prayed that they'd all, if caught in that trapped situation, had a hero like Chet come in to save them.

118

Then again, there was also being prepared. In her mind, now she knew, she was never driving down an old back road she knew nothing about in the middle of a storm. It was too dangerous. But if she was ever, for some odd reason, caught like that again, she was going to make sure her panicking head remembered there were other windows and doors in the vehicle than just the one. And in this vehicle that was the key; she'd have more than two doors. She was also going to order one of those pieces of equipment you could hit the window with and break it. Oh yes, she was going to be prepared.

She got up, took a hot shower, and put her clothes back on, knowing today she had to get some new clothes. So she headed toward the door just as there was a knock. A beautiful woman with long blonde hair and a pretty blue blouse with white jeans smiled the moment April had opened the door. She held an amazing vase full of bright-yellow sunflowers surrounded by small pink and lavender flowers.

"Hello." April's heart skipped a beat as a smile instantly spread across her own face.

"Good morning. I'm Suzie McDermott. I'm married to Tucker from the ranch, and these are for you. They were sent by a certain cowboy...Chet." Her smile widened. "He asked me to bring them this morning—they're happy flowers. He wanted you to start to have a happy day and I was glad to deliver them this morning and to meet you. The boys called my son Abe last night and were excited that you came out to the ranch and they got to meet you."

"It's so nice to meet you. And I loved meeting all the boys. But flowers—"

"They were just to make you smile, and Chet will be glad they did. He was just disturbed when he came in. After all you'd been through—I'd heard your car is missing—he was thankful he was there to help you."

She swallowed hard. "And, I'm thankful he was too. And I'm completely day confused. I forgot today was Sunday. I had told the boys I would come to church but well, all I have is what I have on and I wore it yesterday. Thank goodness the sweet owner of the inn washed them after Chet brought me in Friday night. But then I wore them yesterday, fed the calf in them." She smiled. "I need new clothes. I woke up with a lot on my mind, and clothes were a part of it. But, I'm alive and the flowers are beautiful." She reached for them and smiled as she looked at the bright, happy colors. He had sent the right message.

"I'm so glad you're good. Chet will be too. He just wanted to send you something to lift you up."

"He helped. I'm happy today, and this radiates what I'm feeling. Thank you. I'm thrilled to be alive. Do you think it will be okay to go to church with these dirty clothes on?"

"I tell you what…I came into town just to bring these to you. He wasn't thinking too clearly yesterday, either, because he wasn't thinking about it being Sunday morning. But I didn't tell him that—I wanted to bring them to you. But we just live right outside of town. Tucker doesn't live on the ranch because he's the sheriff. We look like we're about the same size, so do you like dresses, slacks, jeans? What would you like to wear to church? I'm going to bring you something. What size shoe do you wear? We'll give that a try too."

"That's so nice of you. What do y'all wear to church? Is it a real dressy church—you just bring me what you think. I appreciate you so much. It won't make you late?"

Suzie smiled. "I'm thrilled to help. And it's only eight—church starts at ten forty-five. So you head over there and have breakfast, and I'll be back soon. And if you're not here, I will—"

"I'll be here. I'll just get a breakfast sandwich to go and a coffee. I saw one yesterday, and it looked great."

"Coffee…you sound like me—gotta have that. I'll be back."

And then she turned and walked away, and April just stood there, staring at the lovely flowers and thinking what else could show her that there was nothing about being here in this town that was sad. She'd almost died and now she was in a wonderful place.

Of course she knew trouble could come, but right now she would not concentrate on any of that. She was going to get coffee and a breakfast sandwich, and come back here and wait for that beautiful woman to bring her something to wear. And she was going to church.

CHAPTER TEN

Chet had asked Suzie to deliver flowers on Sunday! The moment he woke up, it hit him what he had done. Instantly, he picked up the phone, then realized it was only six in the morning, so, just in case she slept a bit later on Sunday mornings, he didn't call. So he waited until eight but didn't get her, so after thirty minutes he called once more. Thankfully, she picked up.

"I am so sorry! I forgot today was Sunday when I asked you to deliver those flowers. Don't worry about it—deliver them tomorrow. I'm sorry."

She chuckled. "I knew what today was and decided that they needed to be delivered today. I've already done it. Just now coming out of the hotel. She is so very nice, and I'm really glad you asked me to put some happy flowers together. I got to meet her and she, like you, was on the wrong day, and it makes sense—you two had a wild weekend with what y'all went through. But I'm glad I went because she had promised the boys that she would be at church and, I think yesterday was upsetting to her after you telling her about the car. She still has no clothes since they were lost in the accident, so I'm heading to my house to grab her some of mine. Then I'm going to tell her she can ride with me and Tucker to church."

"Thank you. I wasn't thinking again." His brain had obviously gone bonkers.

"I'm glad to do it. She told me she was really stressed, and that's why she didn't go shopping but stayed in her room. But, I think you should know, she seemed much better. She was smiling and eager to come to church—not just because she told the boys she would be there but because she wants to be. So, I think it's okay…you can relax."

He swallowed the log in his throat. *Why was he feeling so emotional?* "Thanks. So, I'll see y'all at church."

"That will be great. And Chet, sometimes when you have something horrible in your life, the good moments are illuminated. I think that's what she was feeling this morning. She lived. She lived because of you. And I want to thank you for that. You went in there and did good."

They finished the call and he got busy, needed to be busy. First, he had to go to the barn and check on the calf to make sure she was making progress. He knew the boys were taking care of business but he still needed to check on the calf's health. By the time he got back to the house and got dressed, he was excited to get to church. So were the boys at breakfast, because they had obviously decided they really liked her. He was just glad she was okay and such a nice person. And that he'd been there when she'd needed him.

But there was nothing else there.

Nothing.

He pulled into the church parking lot, not far behind Tucker. He tried to excuse the way his heartbeat picked up just from knowing April was in the back seat. When he pulled in, he purposefully parked beside Tucker. He got out and walked around the end of his truck just as Abe jumped from the passenger door on the other side, yelled hello, and took off in the direction of the other boys. Chet headed for the other passenger door, telling himself he needed to back off, but he didn't listen. His boots kept walking, and there was nothing he could do about it.

Tucker got out just as he made it up along the back end of the truck and reached for the door handle. "Whatcha doin'?"

"I just thought I'd open the door for April," he said as he did exactly that…and found the seat was empty. He looked at Tucker—who was grinning.

"When my pretty wife took her some clothes and offered for us to come back and pick her up, Mabel was there and said she wanted to bring her. So she's not with us. But if you look in that direction—I've never seen her, but heard she had pretty long hair the color of cinnamon toast, according to the boys—the lady's hair with her back to us talking to the ladies, Chili, and Drewbaker matches their description."

Chet looked up the slightly angled hillside and yes, there she stood. Standing there with Mabel, Miss Jo, Nana, and, of all people, Chili and Drewbaker. They were all laughing, and he could only imagine what they were laughing about. They might be a small crowd of older people but you never knew what they were up to, especially those two men who loved retirement and were usually on the bench outside the diner carving on things or inside eating and having a good time, talking to everyone.

You never knew what they were going to be talking about. They had been out of town yesterday and Friday, so they hadn't been here for the drama he and April had been through. Until today. They had gone fishing a few days, and obviously had gotten back last night. They probably had fishing tales to tell, and so April was hearing their stories and it looked like she was having a good time.

Suzie got out and looked at him, eyes twinkling. "She's developing a fan club, it looks like."

"Looks that way," Tucker agreed with a grin. "Go on over there and see how she's doing. Suzie told me she had taken it hard yesterday, but has made peace with it this morning. I have a feeling she'll be glad to see you and to let you know she's alright because of you."

April's golden sun-kissed eyes sparkled and though he didn't want to admit it, he knew Tucker was probably right. They would be forever connected through that accident. "Okay, I'll head that way. I'm glad she's okay, and thanks for telling me. It helped me to relax this morning instead of continuing to worry about her."

He wasn't sure why he'd said so much. Everyone didn't need to know he was worried about her. This town was getting to be on the matchmaking side, and he'd sidestepped it so far and had no plans to get caught up in it now.

Putting that behind him, he started up the slight incline toward the group, his eyes stuck on her pretty brunette hair. He heard the guys all the way from the back of the church having a good time before the church service started, playing basketball on the concrete slab or just enjoying being together with their friends from town. But his focus was on April.

"Well, thar you are. It's good to see you this mornin', Mr. Hero," Drewbaker greeted him, his bushy brows raised.

"Yep, folks are talkin'. Excitement is boilin' over about what you did to save this here *beeu*-uty," Chili declared. "We wouldn't have enjoyed hunting fer a car knowing she was trapped inside. You did good."

"Yes, you did." Miss Jo moved over and wrapped her arm around his waist. A short little gal, she barely came up to his chest.

He grinned down at her, this woman who had always welcomed the new boys with an open heart and pie. "I was glad to be the one God put there to help her." His gaze automatically lifted from smiling Miss Jo to April. His heart did a lunge, and he felt it all the way down to his toes as those beautiful sparkling golden eyes touched his. It was almost like a gentle caress, there was so much emotion in them.

"Thank you, Chet," she said, her words causing more chaos inside him. "But I dealt with it. And I focused on what you said and on the fact that I was alive.

And now, I'm here to celebrate." She smiled, and it radiated through him. "You should have seen the boys. They got here right before I did and," her eyes teared up, "they all came up and gave me a hug. And told me they had enjoyed seeing me and that they knew that God had sent you to save me. And they really seemed excited about that."

Her words drilled through him. His stomach churned and his heart began a rapid beat. He wasn't sure what exactly was going on. "I'm glad He used me," he managed.

"We all are," Mabel said. "So what do you think about her pretty outfit?" She grinned as she waved her hand down the length of April.

She had on a soft pink flowing blouse that set off her pretty lips and hair…and those dazzling eyes. She wore a pair of white jeans and a pair of sandals; his gaze had swept down her and lingered on her sandals. They looked as if they might be a bit large for her feet but, still, her toes and her feet were pretty. Odd, he didn't normally notice women's feet. Then again, he knew he noticed everything about this woman. And he was going to have to fight that.

He lifted his gaze and met those eyes again. "You look really nice. I talked to…to Suzie." He stumbled over his words. "I called to apologize to her for calling the flowers in for delivery today. We had a rough two days, and my days got mixed up. But she said it was great, that she was glad to meet you and was able to loan you some clothes."

Her smile bloomed wider. "Yes, and we wear the same size, so that worked out perfect. My feet are a bit smaller but no worries, I'm wearing them anyway, so y'all watch out. If I trip, please try to catch me." Her laughing words got chuckles and laughter out of everyone.

"I can guarantee you someone will try to catch you," Nana said. "All my boys came for breakfast this morning and you were the topic of all conversation. They are really excited that you're here and might go on the roundup with them. If you come out and go with the boys," she looked at her grandson. "Chet, would you take April for a horse ride this week to make sure she rides good enough for a roundup?"

His mouth went dry as he nodded; then he found his words. "Yes, I can do that."

"Great. Is that okay with you?" she asked April.

He watched what he thought was hesitation in April's nod. "Yes. I've never ridden much. But I want to do this since the fellas really seem like they want me to. So yes, if you don't mind, Chet, that would be nice."

He did not miss that everyone was smiling. "How

about Tuesday? I don't want to take up your Sunday—
that would be three days in a row—so let's do Tuesday,
if it works for you. I need to go do some things, anyway.
How does that sound?" He was rambling. Today would
have been a great day to take her riding, but *he* needed
to put space and some time between them. And he and
some others were riding down river looking for her car.
He didn't tell her that, not wanting her to want to ride
along. He really needed some distance before he took
her out horse riding, just the two of them. Yeah, he
needed at least two days to get ready for just the two of
them. He was stuck on the number two. Maybe he
should have said Wednesday and got a three in there,
but the roundup was on Friday, so he needed time in
case he had to take her out again to make sure she was
okay. He had to get whatever was going on in his crazy
head straight.

"That sounds good. I have some things I have to
take care of tomorrow. I'm getting me a rental delivered
tomorrow until I can go buy my own new SUV. I called
before I came to church."

He smiled while everyone's smiles widened.

Chili grinned. "She was telling us how she was in a
cute little Mercedes. Those are some pretty little cars
that run real good and are really classy but obviously
didn't go over our flooded country roads too good, so

an SUV will be better. Me and Drewbaker and all these cowboys like trucks, but an SUV will work."

"Yes," Nana agreed, her gaze locking with Chili's for a brief moment. "It'll give you more room for carrying more than a suitcase and a computer bag."

Chet listened as everyone commented on that. She'd mentioned to him that she traveled, and obviously she'd talked with all of them about it too. And they seemed as if they'd enjoyed hearing about her trips, with the questions and smiles. Looking at them all, they seemed like they all knew her really well.

He needed to move, get his head back on straight so he'd stop wishing he knew her well.

"Okay, Tuesday. I need to head on in, and since I have your number, I'll call you about what time I can pick you up."

"Thanks, but I'll have a vehicle and can drive out."

"Great." He knew everyone was looking at him, but all he could see was her smile. And that's all he kept seeing as he walked away and headed toward the church entrance. The preacher stood at the door. He was a cowboy himself and wore his boots, jeans, and a Western shirt. He fit in. His name was Luke Walters, but they called him Preacher.

"Mornin', Chet. I hear we have some celebrating to do. I hear you are a hero."

"Well, I guess I should just say God used me, and I'm glad He did."

Preacher nodded. "Yes, it's always a privilege when you know directly that you were used. I'm glad you were there, too. And she seems like a nice lady."

He nodded. "Yes, and I think the town likes her." And then he walked inside. He needed distance.

He didn't need to talk about April all the time. Nope, he did not.

CHAPTER ELEVEN

Monday morning came, and April was walking down the sidewalk to the Jeans And Things store that the ladies had told her was owned by a fairly new gal in town—the granddaughter of one of the ladies at church. She had met a lot of people yesterday at church but not the grandmother or the owner of the store. They'd said Emmy was out of town on family business and wouldn't be home until late last night. But, they'd been sure to inform her that she'd left a note on her door that said she'd be back today, first thing.

It was funny how everyone knew everything. Just thinking about it made her smile. She had eaten a muffin from the coffee bar this morning and was there when her credit card arrived by special delivery. She was very thankful as she took the package, with Mabel smiling.

The woman told her there was no hurry on paying her when April had pulled the card out and held it out to her to process her room charge. April had insisted and Mabel grinned then processed the payment.

"I hear you're going out to ride with Chet tomorrow," she'd said as she finished.

That had straightened April's laughter right out as she'd grabbed a firm grip on herself and said it was strictly because the boys wanted her on the cattle roundup. And it was.

At least that was what she was telling herself as she now reached the clothing store. Shopping wasn't her favorite thing; she was an odd woman since most women loved shopping. She preferred sitting at a desk and typing out a new book. And that was why she'd also ordered a new laptop computer, because she knew she was ready to start working on the story that was building in her head. And this idea that was brewing didn't seem like it was for her character who solved crimes and then moved on. No, this was something different. And, of course, she couldn't use all the kids, but she'd figure out something. In her heart of hearts, she knew it was going to be something new and different for her but good. All she needed was her fingers on the keyboard and the magic would happen.

But right now, she needed clothes. Thankfully,

sweet Suzie had brought her not just the outfit for church but another pair of jeans and a cute, colorful orange T-shirt that looked good with her hair. She'd told her if Jeans And Things didn't have all she wanted, there was another store down the street at the hair salon. The older woman who owned the hair salon always enjoyed having the clothing to tempt her customers with, but it might be a little older style than she was looking for. Ruth was nearly eighty and still loved doing hair but had started looking for someone who might want to come in with her.

What had hit April when Mabel had told her about Ruth was that she was nearly eighty and still wanted to do hair every day. April had no worry about knowing she wore her hair straight because she had no desire to fix a hairdo every day. No, she liked the freedom of it hanging down or being up in a ponytail when she was deep in the words of a book. But one thing she knew: she was going down to Ruth's Hair Salon and Getup because she wanted to meet this lady. She was smiling just thinking about her and the character. Just the thought of her was inspiring in her brain.

She reached the heavy wooden door of Jeans And Things and pulled it open, causing a jingle to announce her entrance.

A woman with a head of warm brown hair looked

up from where she was dressing a mannequin and gave a bubbly smile. They were about the same age but that smile made April excited she'd come. And the mannequin was getting a great outfit: a red blouse that came down to the hips of her linen pants.

"Good morning. I'm Emmy Swanson, how are you today? I got back into town last night but this morning went over to the diner and got a cup of coffee and a cherry strudel for breakfast and heard that I was going to have a visitor."

"They're wonderful over there. I'm April Mallory and so glad to be here."

"After what you went through I'm glad you're alive and doing good."

April nodded. "Me too. And so glad you have clothes since I don't. The ladies are a hundred percent behind you and the other store. And I'm so glad you're here, because I need clothes. I'm a bit of a strange person, I don't keep a lot of things. I own a few that will fit in my suitcase, which that, too, I'll be looking for."

Emmy cocked her head. "Seriously, you live out of your trunk?"

"Well, not really—just carry my suitcase from one hotel or cabin to the other. I have a vehicle, a suitcase of clothes, and a computer, and I travel. It may sound weird but that's just how I live. I don't put roots down, and I love it that way. I have to say, this is a great town and I'll probably be here a month. Everyone is so nice. And the boys at the ranch are wonderful. Which reminds me, I'm going on a roundup with them and will need jeans. I'm glad to see you have shoes, if there are any in my size."

Emmy grinned. "They got ya. They are good at that, I hear. I haven't lived here all that long—about a year ago, I moved to town. But I leave most weekends to go see…family, and haven't really gotten to know the boys that much. I own a women's store, so they aren't in here."

The way she'd said *family* had a bit of an odd sound to it but April didn't go there. "I am content with the way I live. I see the world and write about it." She didn't say fiction but she almost did. "I use it as an excuse to research things. I love the way I live. I see the United States and other places every once in a while, with an opened eye view. Then I move on when I feel like it. I've never had an adventure like I did upon entering this little town, but I'm glad to be here. And I can tell by just what I see at a glance that I'm going to love your store and be thankful that with one—no, two—stops with the other store in town that I can fill up a suitcase."

"Well, that's inspiring," Emmy said, eyes

twinkling. "I'll be glad to help you fill up your suitcase, and I can assure you that Ruth will love it too. So, come on, let's have an adventure and get you suited up."

April liked this woman. "Sounds perfect." And then they did exactly that; they shopped and had fun doing it. And she got a pair of boots—cowgirl boots, something she'd never had before.

And she loved them.

* * *

Chet sighed as he looked at the cloudy sky. He'd just finished the book by B.P. Joel, he'd needed a distraction the last few nights, since not finding the car he and his brothers and ranch hands had searched for over the last few days. He was now, more than ever relieved that he'd been on that road on that dark rainy night to pull her out of that doomed car. His thoughts had been flooded thinking of what could have happened and B. P. Joel had helped him. The man could write, and his book had distracted Chet a little from the woman who, try as he might, he couldn't get off his mind.

He'd ordered another couple of books by the new-to-him author and hoped they were on his doorstep when he got home tonight. After today, he was going to need more distraction, and there was no way he could deny it. Spending the morning with April was going to be… complicated.

It was strange how the writer—no, not the writer but the main character, a woman named Tullie—made him think of April, but for some reason he couldn't place. Even stranger, though: the same character and the way she thought and the path she'd chosen at the end of the book was so close to being him, it was weird. She walked away from the personal relationship he'd thought had developed between her and the man who had helped her solve the crime, she had decided she couldn't commit. He would have done the same thing…walked away.

When he went online to order the next book, he saw the same female character was the main character of all the stories; that had him curious to see how the next books went so he ordered two books.

But now, he stood at the entrance of the barn and studied the sky. It looked like it could rain again but he hoped it held off because he needed to make sure April could ride.

But as he studied it he knew it could be a storm brewing. Hopefully it would hold off. Maybe the clouds would pass over them and the rain would happen somewhere else in the county. The ranch was so large that it got parts of it, thank goodness, and they would move some cows to feed off the grass the rain kept alive. That was part of the reason for their herding cattle Friday. To make sure that the grass that was growing in certain spots was getting used.

Plus, they'd found the cattle seemed to enjoy being moved around—kept them from getting bored. He liked moving around like that, too. If he had to check the same fences in the same pastures all the time, he'd be bored, and he felt like cattle might feel the same way. He was crazy, and he knew it, but that was the way it was.

He turned and headed back into the barn from where he checked the weather. He headed toward the stalls that held his horse and Cupcake, the really reliable horse when it came to trusting one with a new rider. He wouldn't have to worry about April. They would ride a different direction than what he'd originally planned, just in case it rained. They'd ride toward the river, and there were places to hole up for a while if they did happen to get rain.

He'd called April to see whether he needed to pick her up, but she'd been happy to say that she had an SUV delivered last night and she'd be out at eight, the time he'd told her would be best. That way, if he really needed to coach her, they'd have time. Plus, he was thankful the boys were all in school. He had endured their questions during breakfast because they knew their now favorite person was coming to ride. They went through phases like that. It had been Jolie, then Lucy, then Suzie, and now it looked like it was April. And…he couldn't help that they were smart boys. All four of them were good ladies. The only difference was this one wasn't going to turn out like he feared they were thinking. He wasn't going to worry about that right now.

Despite pushing it aside, he couldn't help but wonder about their reasoning. A guy didn't have to get married or be matched up.

Cupcake watched him as he opened the gate, then flicked her tail as she let Chet saddle her. This was always the horse they let new riders ride because they had no skills or experience. And also those who hadn't ridden in a very long time. Thank goodness when they hired cowhands they had experience on a horse, so Cupcake never got ridden hard. She was nice, calm, and easy to enjoy taking a new rider for a ride. And, she normally stayed in the main pasture, making her life easy until someone new came along who needed her. And today that was April.

After he'd saddled both horses, he led them out to the front of the barn, into the light sunshine peeking from the clouds. He paused as he saw a bright burgundy vehicle, shiny and new, pull up the drive. She was here; he waved so she would see him and come to the big red barn, which she did, stopping just a few steps away from him in her big, safe vehicle.

She climbed out, looking amazing. Like a cowgirl. She had a pair of fancy boots, soft brown leather with a big red leather flower on both sides. Her well-fitting jeans were tucked into them, showing off the boots. She'd been to the main store in town. He knew the ladies enjoyed the store and Emmy, the owner. She also had on a bright-pink tank top that came down over her hips but it was snug and showed how nice her fig— *Okay, whoa, back up.*

There, he'd gotten it out. He jerked his gaze back to her face, seeing that she'd pulled her hair into a ponytail, which only made her golden eyes sparkle more, even though he saw uncertainty in them. Seeing that, he automatically lifted his hand.

What was he going to do with his hand? *Touch her pretty jaw*—no! He reached for his own jaw and rubbed it, realizing he should have shaved. He had a couple of days of growth and it was scroungy. He hoped she didn't mind—*what are you thinking?*

He had gone slap crazy. It didn't matter what she thought about his looks. Whether he had a hairy face or was clean-shaven, it didn't matter. She was here so he could make sure she could ride, to be ready for Friday.

"Good mornin'," he snapped, before he got his tone under control.

She hitched her brow. "Good morning to you too." She closed the door, then placed her hands on her hips.

The woman was…she wasn't the most gorgeous woman alive—he tried to throw that into his thoughts to maybe slap himself in the head. But the truth was she was a beautiful woman with a great smile, amazing eyes, and yeah, pretty in her own special way. There, he'd said it. He'd admitted it and now maybe he could get through the day without going senseless.

He held the reins of her horse out to her. "I've got your horse saddled. This is Cupcake, and she knows how to handle a new rider. Or riders who haven't ridden in a while. She'll take care of you and that way, you can relax. We'll ride this morning so you can do that when there is a lot going on around you like there will be on Friday. We'll have a good day, and I'll see how you handle being on her, and then I'll be able to relax Friday."

"Okay, sounds good. For some reason, you seem a little wary."

Bingo. "Well, one time we had a bit of a problem. That was Suzie. We were herding near the river for a long time and had an unusual bit of cattle trouble and

144

she was thrown in. But today it's just us and I'll be between you and the water."

"What happened?" she asked with genuine curiosity in her tone.

"The horse got scared by a cow blasting from the trees, and her horse bolted and threw her into the very dangerous water. Thankfully, Tucker saved her. That's it. Don't let that scare you. This is a great, mild-mannered horse."

She smiled.

Man, oh man, what a smile.

"I believe you. I promise you that I'll hang on tight. I might not be the best and it's been a while, but I have my boots. Though they are a little more fancy than I need them to be, I like them and they will hang onto those stirrups really well. They were all Emmy had at her store that fit me, so I bought them and here I am. Ready to ride."

"It looks like you'll be set for the reunion party, with the dancing on the street in your fancy boots."

Her smile widened.

Oh goodness.

"Is that so? That's nice to know. I'll wear them, and it's going to be great when I write about—in my articles about them."

He was really curious about her articles.

Why was it that sometimes when she started to talk about her work, she shut up quickly? It was strange. Later, he might ask her about it, but right now they had riding to do, and that was his priority—not asking her personal questions about things he didn't need to know. Things that might stir his interest more than it already was stirred, going as wild as a river being churned up by a tornado.

Yep, he needed to keep this all about getting her ready to ride on Friday. And that was it.

CHAPTER TWELVE

They had ridden for a while and his mind rolled. Finally, he let his thoughts out. "Look, you know a lot about me. If I haven't told you since rescuing you from that car in that flood, then the boys here at the ranch have told you. Or who knows…the ladies at the diner. Or even Mabel, at the inn where you're staying. But you're new here and you're expecting all this stuff from me, but you have said almost nothing. You write articles, so you say, and you don't live anywhere. You live out of a suitcase and what used to be that little tiny car that you almost drowned in when I pulled you out of that river. And yet you have said nothing else about your history. Despite that, you want to know everything about me—I want to know more about you. What exactly do you write?"

She looked over at him from her horse, which she was doing good on. Yes, he had given her the best horse in the world, made exactly for people who weren't used to riding. But it wasn't riding on the horse that made her suddenly look uncomfortable; it was his question. And that made him want to know even more. *What was her story?*

"Chet, I, honestly…" She paused, and that look in those beautiful eyes really had him wondering what was going on in that mind of hers.

"Come on, what? You just don't have any family? You know mine died in the car wreck that brought me here to this wonderful, humongous ranch for kids with no one, and now I've made myself part of it and I'm going to live the rest of my life here helping all these other guys who you're going to get to know better on our cattle drive. So what is it about this bunch of boys who are excited to see you ride with them, the new lady in town who has somehow stolen their hearts in just two meetings? My question is what's *your* story? What brought you here?" He seriously wanted to know, not just for him but for the boys, He was their protector and he would do it even if it involved a beautiful woman.

Her expression tightened, her eyes darkened. "Why do you suddenly sound like I'm here to cause harm? Or, looking for a matchup? I'm never calling anyplace home, so no worries."

"I didn't mean that." Something wasn't right; he knew it. "Look, I'm going to die a single man, a man with no holds on me, no responsibility to any person—" His mind whirled as he thought of what the boys might be hoping when they'd invited her to herd the cattle. But no matter how much he knew all them looked up to him and might be thinking they were going to matchmake him, they wouldn't. And what he'd just told her was the reason.

But that didn't stop him from wanting to know more about her because if he could help her, that was what he lived to do—help people.

"Why do you say that? You want to know about me then tell me why you are saying what you're saying."

They stared at each other. He'd lost track of the conversation as he got lost in those eyes that were now digging into him with fierce challenge. So be it. "I was a kid who wasn't able to help my parents in the fight they were having while driving down a flooding road. I lived through the horrible tragedy of the flood clinging to a tree as my lifeline—and it was that—God watched out over me. He gave me strength to hold onto the tree while my parents died in the car downstream. I lived and found my destiny here on this ranch, watching the McDermott's help me and others like me all these years.

I grew up wanting, knowing and determined to do the same for others. I just feel like there is something wrong in your life, that there is a reason you won't settle down somewhere and travel all the time. Even I call a place home, but why don't you want to call some place home?" His words slammed into him as he instantly thought of Tullie, the main character in B. P. Joel's book. She wouldn't settle down, she would call no place home.

April's expression had softened as he spoke but her eyes looked pained. "I'm so sorry you went through that. And that's wonderful that you're using your experience to help the boys. I can see how much it works just in the expressions of the boys when they talk about you or watch you. But... I don't talk about my past."

"I don't either, normally. But I think you need to know that I have a feeling the boys think I could be like my McDermott brothers and find love one day. But I'm never going to let myself fall in love, even though the both of us know that we're attracted to each other. But now you know I lost everybody in my life as a boy and I'll never risk going through that again. I came here after so much trauma and other foster homes before they sent me to the ranch, where usually boys come who haven't made it somewhere else, or they think this would be the best place for them. They were right about me and all the other boys here, and that's what I'm going to do—I'm going to help the other boys who have gone through kind of what I've been through in other ways. But my curiosity is, April, why does something tell me that you and I have something in common?"

He had probably just shot it all to heck but what did it matter? He had made it totally clear to her that there would never be anything between him or any woman. It didn't matter whether he was attracted to them or not; he wasn't going to allow that to happen to himself. He wasn't going to ever live through what he lived through, losing his mom and dad after riding in the back seat hearing them yell at each other. And while his father found out his mom was having an affair, he found it out too, and found out that she wanted a divorce. He had been young, and some of the last words he had heard before that river swept them off that road and into what became his nightmare even more was his dad asking her why, and she had told him because he hadn't made her happy.

"You're right," April said, softly. "I have a past that I'm not comfortable with. A past that makes me determined to always remain single like you. To never, *ever* depend on anyone but myself. To be honest—let me take that back...I'm honestly never completely honest. And part of that comes from something similar to you—I found out at an early age, before something horrible happened in my life, that everything I knew about myself was not true. That everything that I knew about my mother and dad was not true. I've never told anyone that. So I don't know for sure if I'll tell you anything more, but does that help you realize that I came here because I was looking for something? I came here and found what I was hoping I would find—that there are many articles that I could write about the wonderful Sunrise Ranch." She pulled her horse to a halt, not that it took much considering Cupcake was ridden like that often; she just came easily to a stop and so did Chet on Lightning.

"And…"

"And what?" April stared at him but in her mind she was staring at herself point-blank. *Why had she told him that?* She hadn't told anyone that. She wasn't who she thought she was, and she wasn't who she'd been told she was. She had been lied to by her parents until their deaths and then lied to from the shelters, the homes that she was put in. She hadn't known her real name, or she had learned her real name and chosen not to go by it.

"There's more but something is going on in that head of yours. You tend to disappear when you get deep in thought." Chet had his one hand on the saddle horn and his other hand holding the reins crossed over it as he sat in a relaxed manner, studying her. And seeing her, she realized. Seeing everything, pretty much.

"I get caught up in my thoughts sometimes. But we're supposed to be riding and making sure I'd be good enough for the cattle herding on Friday."

"And I've already figured out that you're going to be fine. Our little horse there is doing good. She knew when you wanted to stop and I'm quite certain that when you're ready to start up again, you'll click those boot heels on her side there gently and she'll move forward. Knowing how to stop and start her is basically the important part. We're going to go over this hill and let you look at the river. We're not going to get close enough to it, just in case you decide to go crazy and kick her real hard so she'll run or something comes out and scares her. We don't want anything to happen to you like what happened to Suzie. We were very blessed, I'd say, that she had lived through that but I don't want to take any chances."

Just the way he said those words made something inside her yank hard and yearn. *Yearn*—what a word. She wasn't going to *yearn* for anything. Especially not this amazing man who had saved her life in the river and was now trying to find out what she was hiding. Little did he know that she had hidden her entire life.

Basically, the real her hadn't even been brought out

because she hadn't known as a child she was living a lie and she never stopped once she'd known the truth. But as she stared into those amazing eyes of his, something inside her wanted to tell him who she really was—or who she could be, if she ever let the real person out.

But instead of answering, she clicked her heels against the horse's side, and instantly Cupcake moved forward. He did the same thing. They topped the hill, and her gasp came out all on its own.

"Yeah, it's a beautiful sight, isn't it? Flows through this ranch along with a few other large creeks. Back behind Jolie and Morgan's house is the big river, as rough as it gets, it's tough, but for a kayaker like her it's just a pretty site. And for Morgan, who had dealt with her leaving him and choosing competition kayaking over him, I think he built the house there so he could always remember their times there. Then she came back and everything worked out and now they love it together."

He paused as she looked at him, and his gaze lifted as he looked at the dark cloud rolling in their direction.

"Do you think that's going to come in?"

"Maybe. It's churning but…" He looked at her. "Sometimes the storm is brewing and it blasts out, lets everything loose, and sometimes a storm is brewing and it just stays brewing and it doesn't release." His gaze dug deep.

The man was driving her insane. And yet he was the first person ever to see that there was more to her than the stranger who came in and out of towns and never stayed long enough to have anybody see inside her. Goodness, she had been here a total of— She rolled days through her head, counting. Her accident had been on Friday; she had gone to breakfast on Saturday with him, Tony, and Micah. Then helped them feed the calf. On Sunday she'd gone to church, and met Suzie and the older ladies who set her up for a ride with this cowboy so she'd be ready for this coming Friday. And now it was Tuesday. She had known this man two days short of a week. And he seemed to be looking inside her. "So, uh, if the storm comes in, what are we going to do? Turn around and go back to the ranch?"

His lip hitched up on the right side and his eyes underneath that straw hat cinched downward, and she had a crazy, insane want to place her hand against that bristle on his jaw. She was losing it, period.

"We're going to keep going. And if a shower or a rainstorm comes, there's actually a dirt road not too far away. But before we get to the dirt road, there's a cabin we can find shelter in."

"I'd rather get the adventure going than sit here and get questioned."

"Then here we go. And remember—you stay on that side; I stay between you and that water as we go down the hill."

"Believe me, I'll stay here because I have no desire to go swimming in a rushing river again and you having to come in after me. One time is enough. I'm thankful you came in after me but I don't want to chance either one of us getting hurt this time."

"And we are in agreement on that. But just so you know, if you went in, I *would* come in after you."

Her heart squeezed tight. So tight she almost gasped because she had never, ever had anyone willing to do that for her… other than her parents. She pushed that thought from her mind.

Move forward. Stop looking back.

* * *

Chet liked that April really wanted to ride. He didn't like that he was pressuring hard for her to let him into her world. *Why was he doing that? He wasn't going there, so what was his problem?*

Keeping his mouth shut as they topped the hill that overlooked the river, he let her enjoy it. He remembered the first time he rode here on top of this ridge, overlooking that pretty river as it moved slowly toward the cabin not too terribly far away. The cabin he had decided one day, if possible, he would live in.

Just as he thought that, with no warning, a downpour let loose. She gasped next to him as it was as if God had poured a swimming pool-sized bucket on top of them and it wasn't stopping.

"Okay, I guess it started," he said through the rain, not really minding getting wet. He had been in a lot of cattle herding where it had been normal being drenched but he honestly wanted to smile at her shock. And then, much to his amazement, she started to laugh.

"This is wild. I guess my trip here is meant for me to stay soaking wet the whole time." She chuckled as rain poured all over her, and drenched her hair and her clothes quickly. But she was smiling.

And he was too. "Okay, have fun but follow me— stay on that side of me. Horses don't mind rain. They've walked in it, herded cattle through many rainstorms, so it's all right. It's not far to go to the cabin that I was telling you about." They rode and continued to be drenched. He looked at the sky; it wasn't giving up. He wasn't sure what she was going to say when she got to the cabin, but at least she could get dry and relax.

They rounded the bend, and there where the water had come down and they were no longer on the ridge was his cabin. It had a huge back porch he'd built himself and wide windows that he had installed instead of the small ones that had been in the original cabin. And it had an area on the front that he'd widened, made larger so it really wasn't the tiny cabin it had started out as. It was his home—his official home, the one he had built, the land that he loved surrounding it, and the promise from Randolph that it was always his, as long as he wanted it.

"It's beautiful. Look at that back porch. Obviously y'all use it a lot, and it is a cabin."

They reached the railing that was under a wooden shelter he had built for horses. He led the way as she followed. He quickly dismounted, tied his horse up where it wouldn't get hit by rain, and then he walked over to her side and held his hand up. "All right, let me help you down." He had intentionally avoided her talk about the cabin, though he liked her vision of it.

She took his hand and once again that sizzle ran through him. He wished hard he could put that fire out, but he didn't have time for that as he gripped her hand to help her down. She shifted, pulled her leg over as she stood on the one leg, and just to steady her, he placed his other hand on her waist and held her steady as she lowered to the ground but as she pulled her boot from the stirrup, it hung and she stumbled against him. His arm wrapped around her waist as he let go of her hand

and pulled her booted foot from the stirrup. She was stable, standing solidly on the ground but his arm didn't loosen.

They stood close, steady against each other, it had been this way the night he'd rescued her, but there hadn't been this erratic pounding of his heart, the draw of her pounding heart against his, or the look in her eyes that clung to his, not from fear this time but from... Thinking gone, his gaze dropped to her lips; his arm held her tighter and his head dipped as she leaned into him.

What are you doing?

His lips almost brushed her's before he pulled away, her stunned eyes locked with his and she stepped from his hold.

He fought to be normal. "You're okay. Let me tie your horse." He turned and did just that as thoughts bombarded him about what he'd almost done. He tied her horse to the rail next to his, then took her hand again—for safety, nothing else, he told himself as the feel of her hand sent electric shockwaves through him as he led the way toward his cabin.

The rain pounded them as they walked; no need to run—they were already drenched, and he needed the downpour to clear his head. They stepped up onto the wooden porch and then he opened the door and pushed it into the house. "After you."

He released her hand—forcing himself to do so. He didn't like that he wanted to hold it and didn't like that he had to make himself let go. It was confusing.

She had stopped on his entrance rug that protected his wooden floors from the water and gazed around the room he had made large by knocking out the wall between the kitchen and living room. It was a wide open space with an old stone fireplace that had been put in by the original builder.

"This is awesome. It looks like someone lives here."

"Well, actually, this is my house. I came this direction just because I knew if it rained we'd be safe here, and I wanted to make sure you didn't have to stay out in that. If we had gone in the direction I originally planned, there was nothing but a few trees we could have hidden under and a few cut-out cave type areas, so I decided that you might not really want to do that. I made this choice—I hope it doesn't make you mad."

She was staring at him, her eyes so beautiful. The gold glistening darkened. "No, you made the right choice. We've both been through enough rough water and slogging rain. But, um, so what's the plan?"

"Well, right here—" He turned to the cabinet behind the door and opened it. It was where he specifically kept towels so he would have them for episodes just like this, for himself or if a cowboy happened to be with him. And they weren't regular towels; they were big, teal-toned beach towels that he had found. He pulled one out and before handing one to her, he said, "If you sit on that wooden stool right there on the other side of the door, you can take your boots off. And don't worry—this rug is thick…it's catching all that."

She sat and looked up at him, a big grin spread across her face. He liked it.

She ran her fingers over the varnished wooden seat of the stool. "You are obviously prepared for this kind of entrance. I guess when you're herding cows or you're out there and you come back, you are definitely prepared."

"Yeah. So if you'll pull those boots off…" he said as he placed the towel beside her on the edge of the stool. He looked at her pretty new boots. "We'll get them off, and then we'll dry them. I have a boot dryer that we'll put them over. We'll latch them over the top of that and it will blow warm air inside, and they'll be dry before you know it and ready for that dance."

She reached for her boots, propping her leg on top of her knee, and started to pull. "I am amazed. You have thought of everything. It's interesting and good to know.

I might use—" She stumbled on her words, pausing on working on getting her boot off.

And he was curious.

"I, uh, need all kinds of information for my articles. Who knows—I might write an article if you get stuck in the rain how to get your boots off and get them dry."

He laughed. "Okay. Again, I'm still interested in what you write. You drive me a little bit crazy if you can actually write an article and put that in it and get paid for it."

Her eyes met his, and she then looked back down at the boot and tugged it off, concentrating on it because wet feet and boots didn't always just slide right off. She got it off before he offered to help, but he had a feeling she would tell him no, thank you.

She got the other one off, reached for the towel and stood up. "That's a wonderful stool, beautiful and rustic," she said as he sat down where she'd been and grabbed one of his boots to remove.

"Thanks, I should have made it big enough for two."

"You *made* that stool too?"

"Yeah. Believe me, around here, we learn to do a lot of stuff. It may not be big and fancy, but it fits in with my cabin home and I like it." He didn't say it was ragged and renewed, but that's how he looked at it.

To his surprise, she turned slightly away from him as he pulled his boots off and from the side view he had, she seemed to study the room. He grabbed his towel, wrapped it around his soaked pants, and then moved to stand beside her. He realized she was staring at his bookshelf, which was across the room beside his tan leather lounge chair. On the table next to it was his recently finished book by B.P. Joel. He looked back at her and saw she had a strange look on her face.

She lifted her gaze to his. "You," she said, her voice low, "like to read?" The last part was odd sounding, as if she forced it to sound like nothing had happened. But something had.

"Yeah. And the book over there is the author whose next two books I'm hoping get delivered soon. I just finished his first book and I'm ready for more. This first one I told you earlier is that one on the table. It was great."

"I'm glad you enjoyed it—" She spun away suddenly. "Um, do you have any dry clothes I could wear?"

I'm glad you enjoyed it... Her words hung in the air. And she seemed jumpy as she turned away from him. Not sure what had happened, he walked past her toward the hallway. "This way, and I'll get you something to wear while I put yours in the dryer." He led the way down the small hall to the bathroom. "I'll be right back with clothes—though they're not going to fit, at least they'll be dry while I toss these in the dryer. You're welcome to take a shower."

She said nothing, just looked around the bathroom. "I'll just wear what you bring me and take a shower at the hotel."

"Whatever you want to do." He turned away and headed to his room for clothes.

Was he crazy, or was she acting odd? What had happened?

CHAPTER THIRTEEN

Moments later, after Chet had handed her a stack of clothes, April stood with her back to the bathroom door and tried to get herself straight. She was thankful she'd managed not to gasp when she spotted his B.P. Joel book on the side table.

Her book.

He was reading her work.

She had purposefully misled everyone by using initials for her name. She hoped he thought he was reading a book by a man.

His words came back to her, about his thoughts about the author he was reading. He'd seen exactly what she was doing—well, almost. *He* had no idea that she was Joel. *B* for Blair, her mother's name, and *P* for Parson, her father's last name—the name that should have been hers but she had never been known by it. Hadn't even known it was hers until after her parents were dead. And she used Joel as her author last name, which had been her dad's first name. Complicated and secretive, but the only connections she had to the person she was supposed to be, but had never known until after she'd lost everyone.

She stood in the bathroom, her head spinning, her pulse roaring. *He was reading her.*

He had been talking about it earlier; he had seen it all! She had to get that through her mind before she went back out there. She stripped off the really wet clothes and handed them around the door where he waited for them.

"Thank you."

"I'll put them in the dryer. Take you time."

And she did. She dried off, pulled on the sweatpants then the T-shirt and finally she pulled on the red plaid, cotton, long-sleeved shirt over her T-shirt. She had on no bra now and was thankful that he'd obviously known she wouldn't be comfortable walking around in a T-shirt, even one too big for her. She greatly appreciated his thoughtfulness.

It also told her that, like her, he wasn't up for temptation.

Neither of them wanted anything between them and

were saying no to the crazy temptation that was between them.

She rubbed her forehead. She wasn't ready to go out there with him, so she looked in the cabinet and thank goodness there was a blow dryer that she hadn't expected to find. She got it out, then took her time as she dried her long, straight, almost bronzed-toned hair with the depth of brown so she couldn't be considered a redhead—though, actually, if the sun hit her hair just right, she appeared to be. Everything about her, even her hair color, was misleading and not straight on. She wasn't brown-headed; she wasn't a redhead: she was an in between—just like she wasn't a Mallory; it was the fake name she'd been raised as, the only name she'd ever really known. She'd filed for it and made it her legal name as soon as she was old enough. She wasn't a Parson; she was a Mallory. All the other names she used as her fake name, not the other way. Confusing, just like she was about her life; it was the same with all the names she'd never known as hers. She'd been a young girl, eight when this had all come out, when she'd been left alone, scared, and confused.

She blew her hair dry, *completely* dry, then she forced herself to open the door and walk out. Unable to help herself—which made her angry—she glanced in the door that was open that led into the bedroom, Chet's room. It was manly; he had a thick cow hide on the floor, a rusty brown mixed with cream white, a certain kind of brand of cow that she had seen in the short time she was here. She had seen some of them running around, so she assumed he helped raise them, fed the world with them, and then used their skin for a beautiful rug. Everything else in the room was manly and Western: he had a tan bed cover and a rusty-red blanket folded at the bottom, and just as she had expected, everything was completely in order.

That was one thing she had feared about herself, if she had to keep house for herself. It was different in a hotel room: somebody came in and straightened up after her. When she got to working on a book, she sat down and got to typing; her mind whirled and keeping things straight was not part of it, so being in a hotel room worked out really great for her. She'd probably have to have a full-time housekeeper if she ever bought a place. But then again, she wrote in silence; she wrote holed up by herself, so someone in the house at the same time might not work. *Why are you thinking these things?*

She had just hesitated and thank goodness he wasn't anywhere where he could see what she had done. She moved forward, out of the hallway. He wasn't in the living room, so she looked to the right, into the kitchen, and there he was, clean, dry, and amazing. He'd changed into pale, worn jeans that fit him well—and why was she looking at them? He wore a T-shirt, white, simple, and yet he looked perfect—and she was crazy! Yes, he was perfect but she didn't have to notice.

He looked up from where he was slicing tomatoes. He didn't say anything at first. His gaze locked with hers; she tried to look away but couldn't.

"I feel better, but will be glad when my clothes get ready. I mean, I don't mind wearing yours but they're a little big."

"I'm glad they're a little big. You're not a real tall person but you're not a short person either. I like the difference in us."

And what did he mean by that, "he liked the difference in them"? Oh, they were different, all right. He was tall, lean, and muscular; she was…well, what the heck—she really liked the way he looked but she wouldn't want to look that way herself. *Change the subject!*

"Your house is really nice."

"Thank you very much. I've worked hard on it. This is my first home and probably will be my only home that I've made myself. So who knows—if I live to be an old, old, old man, which I'm kind of hoping I'll do, there's no telling what will be in this house."

She smiled, unable to stop herself. "I hope you

make it to being an old, old, old man but you'll have to be careful, going and rescuing women who drive down roads they probably shouldn't have driven down."

He lifted his shoulder. "What is meant to be, will be. I'm making us some bacon, lettuce, and tomato sandwiches. Hope you like it. If not, I've got some ham in the fridge and peanut butter, if one of those is better."

"I like BLTs."

"Great. I've got the bacon cooking, and some mayonnaise and fresh tomatoes. I grow them on the side of the house, along with some other things. I've got some fresh watermelon in the icebox if you want some. I tasted it and it's good, but you never know about a melon."

She smiled at the way he said the words, teasing. "Sounds really great. Thank you. This is completely not the day that we had planned, is it?"

"Not at all. I don't mind, though. You know, at least you're safe."

"And you too. You made the right choice, coming this direction."

He smiled. "I would have really been kicking myself in the—well, I'd be kicking myself if we'd taken the other way and had to hide up in a black cave or a weedy, dense line of trees."

"I'm very glad about that too." And she was. "I just

blew-dry my wet hair, and I'm assuming that we're not going back out 'til the sun perks up. Or are you calling someone to come get us since your truck's not here?"

"That wasn't my plan. I thought we'd ride back in when it stops, but if you want somebody to come get you, I can sure do it."

She should say *Call somebody, let me leave now.* "I'm good, I'm...I'm perfectly fine." She turned and walked over to his bookshelf, glancing down at her book. He had finished it and laid it neatly on the table beside him—well, not him but where he sat and read. Where he would read the next two when they were delivered. She knew what the next two books were; she knew that this book had been her first and dealt with deep issues she was having—not her but the main character trying to get over the murder of her parents as a young girl by solving others troubles and making it right for them. This was the book that had sold her main character in the story to the publisher and kept readers' attention. This was the book that had helped save her from the torment inside her and started the sale of every book to this huge company. *This* book had her in it.

Her heart started thundering. This book was actually before she realized she needed to watch how much of herself she put in the book. But most people didn't know her. Would never connect things because of that. But Chet had already connected a little, and he didn't even know she was the author.

"That's an amazing book. I'd give it to you to read but I'm giving it to Micah. I'm expecting the next two in the mail. I might have to put my raincoat on and go out to the mailbox to check."

She looked at him. *Was he serious?* "You'd go out in the rain to get her books—I mean his books?"

He grinned and nodded. "It was that good. He's a talented writer. I started reading books when I was in foster homes and fighting the trauma that I had lived through. Reading helped me disappear into somebody else's story, someone else's trouble. And I always like books where it all came out good. Not a fan of books that don't end well. I lived that." He grinned. "I don't really read romances, *but* if a romance has been introduced in the book, then it should have a happy ending—them getting married, needs to at least be on the horizon. For everyone moving forward is always the right thing. But as much as I liked the book and the bad guy caught I'm not sure B.J. made the right ending in this book. Yes, he solved the who did it, but it ended with readers thinking the main character would never look at that guy again. She walked away. So now I'll see what happens in the next books. Me, I'm always going to move forward. I determined that before I was even young enough to know what it meant. When I was hanging on a tree limb in the middle of a raging river." His eyes held hers and she couldn't breathe.

Struck hard by his words she spun away from him. She had to put her back between them again and pretended to be studying his bookshelf.

She hadn't moved forward.

Yes, she was moving forward in some ways with her writing, her discovering America one move after the next as she wrote her books. But she knew not everything was moving forward. But…it hit her then. "You aren't moving on. Yes, you've moved forward but you're staying here instead of looking for something else. Instead of taking a chance on love." She hadn't even turned to look at him; she kept her back to him. She couldn't let him see anything on her face right now because she couldn't control what he might see. What was wrong with her?

"I had plans maybe at one point that I would move forward—I would go find a new life," he said, his voice low. "But I couldn't, and this ended up being my home. If I hadn't liked it or if I'd have felt drawn to move elsewhere, I would have. A lot of the guys who are coming to the reunion, they've become huge successes in happiness and moving forward. Some of them are still struggling, but most of them are doing great. Some of it just depends on what they went through and, I think, how young it started. And what it was."

Her mind went to Tony. She turned toward him. "Tony—he's really scarred?"

"Yes, but determined to move forward and to him staying here and following in my footsteps is his way of doing that. In all honesty, he's been through more than most of the boys who call this ranch home. He's got scars all over him. Not just scars from cigarettes…"

"That infuriates me," she ground out.

"I'm with you. I looked it up and his dad is dead—somebody killed him. His story was so bad he made the paper. I don't know if Tony's ever seen it, but as far as I can tell, Tony doesn't think about it now. He's made huge progress. You're going to meet Lucy soon. That's our brother Rowdy's wife, who is an artist. She has scars but her scars didn't come from torture—they came from her home fire. She hid them, but Tony saw them, and on his own went and tried to show her that she wasn't the only one dealing with scars. He did the right thing. I wanted him to have a different life, but I'm not going to say anything else to him. If he wants to be here, this will be the place for him, and he'll do other boys a lot of good."

"I think you're right." Everything he said settled over April. This man—and Tony, too—helped other kids who had been hurt in so many different ways than how she had been hurt. But even listening to his story made her think he and the boy were both moving forward in their own way. Moving on, but Chet never planning to marry was like her…she was moving on in her own way, too, and marriage had no place in her future. So why was she still stuck on this?

The rain still pounded down as they settled at the table and made their bacon, lettuce, and tomato sandwiches. He had asked if she wanted hers toasted like his, and she had said yes, and so they had their toasted bread, their thick-sliced homegrown tomato, their green lettuce that he had also grown out there, and the mayonnaise—that he had not made—salt and pepper, and homemade ice tea. They sat in the chairs, not across the table from each other, but he was on the end and she was in the chair beside him. It was a small table, and their elbows almost knocked whenever they were both working on their sandwich.

"This is going to be great. Add a fried green tomato and you'd have made my day," she said as she smiled at him then took a bite.

He smiled and then his brows met, as if he were thinking. "Never had a fried green tomato."

"My mom loved them, said her mom had always made them and she learned it from her mother, so I guess it is one of the only things I know of that…" She paused. *Why was she saying this? Because it's true and it's one of the only things in your life you know your family loved.* "All the women in my life, the ones I never even knew, loved."

He studied her, his eyes gentle. "We might have to get some and try it some time since I've never had one."

She smiled hugely, feeling the support in his words, the understanding that things from the past gave uplifting moments. "Then you're missing out on one of life's best treats. I'll have to make them for you for saving my life."

Chet's smile turned into a delightful chuckle. "I'll have to take you up on that."

Their gazes held for a moment. "Great. It's been awhile but I tend to hold onto things once I love them and I loved my mom, my gram though I never met her, and their green tomatoes so you're in luck."

CHAPTER FOURTEEN

Chet tried not to stare as she told him about the fried green tomatoes. He'd heard of them but never had one and right now, he realized he really wanted to try one. With her. She looked good in his oversized clothing. She'd look good in anything, and he knew it. She'd blown her hair dry, and it glistened in the light. He'd almost kissed her when he'd helped her from her horse and right now he had to fight the want to do it again. The sound of the rain on the metal roof was like a song urging him to wrap his arms around her and see if the memory of her kiss the night he'd rescued her was as unforgettable as it had become in his mind.

Suddenly, she looked up. "Do you think what happened to me on that bridge would happen to anybody else?"

He reached for a piece of bacon, not her. "I hope not. I've been here a long time and it's never happened that way before, so let's hope it doesn't. But like I told you before, I go if I think the bridges are going to be covered."

"Thank goodness you have an instinct to help others. So what exactly about B.P. Joel do you like— other than that, well, I mean, you said you liked it but then you're kinda having confliction about the character?" She took a bite of the sandwich and smiled, even though she had a full mouth. She kept her lips closed and he could tell she liked it.

"He's a talented author, kept my attention. But with that book, it was as if he had been through what the woman, the main character, had gone through. And she was in some way similar to me."

"How was she similar to you?"

Her eyes penetrated his, as if trying to look inside him and as he looked at her, he realized for the first time ever, he wanted to talk about it. "Similar to the way I felt when I realized my parents were killed in the river. They were fighting in their last moments of life. Not so for her parents—they were killed by a man they had testified against and they'd lived all their daughter's life with new names, new fake histories because testifying against the man was something they felt compelled to do. The main character was too young to remember who she was, so her entire life was a lie…that's how the character feels. They were killed by the man they sent to prison and who they had given up their identities for.

"When the bad guy is let loose because of a new crazy law, he found them. He had found their new name through his links, and so he found them and killed them. But the main character lived. Now, years later, she's a detective and she takes on cases and she finds the killer. But for herself, she always walks away because she can't bring herself to be completely happy…can't take that chance, so she walks away and leaves the guy who loved her behind. The book doesn't tell you why but I think she didn't want to have to love and lose—" Chet realized he'd walked right into this as her eyes flashed at those words.

"What about that makes you similar?" she asked, her voice low.

"That's how I am. My parents died that night. I heard their anger, and I'll live hearing it for the rest of my life, knowing that they were going to split up. And that my dad was always going to be torn up because somehow or another he hadn't made my mom happy. She'd gone looking elsewhere. I'm not sure what he did—I was too young to understand, so I don't know what he did to make her feel that way. Me, I'm never putting myself in that position. My life is to help make boys who've been through hard times have a good life. And if I were to marry and go through a hard time and my wife were to walk away from me, what would that prove to these boys I've been trying my hardest to help? It would prove to them that I didn't know what I was talking about and life isn't always what you expect. I want to always be a positive influence for these boys, and I can't trust somebody else to take that and ruin it for me. So that means no wife to one day decide it's over. So in the book, it's different but the same."

She inhaled deeply, silent as she let his words sink in. "I'm sorry that happened to you. I really am, but I'll be honest with you. I very seldom have a conversation like—well, not very seldom. I've never had a conversation like this with anyone. But you're being a wonderful blessing to these boys. You're a good example. I can't imagine if you were to ever fall in love, a woman doing to you what your mom thought your dad did to her—whether we know what happened or whether we know in reality he was neglecting her and didn't realize it or if she was just looking for an excuse to have an affair and fall in love with someone else...that's just something that, um, we'll never know—but you understand that and if you ever went into a relationship, you would guard against that, you know what I'm saying?"

Chet couldn't not stare at her as her words hit deep. Yeah, her words looked inside him and they were absolutely correct. He would never neglect someone; he loved all these boys, his new brothers Morgan, Rowdy, and Tucker, and all the people here. He would never do anything that would be a negative to them, and she saw that—*wow.* "Well, I have to say you're right. I would never do that. But I still can't help but wonder if my dad did it without knowing. I mean, if my mom really was serious, my dad had no idea. I wouldn't want to be that way."

Her stunning smile deepened and her eyes gentled as she slightly bent her head to the side and looked at him.

"You wouldn't do that, I can tell you. You're a guy who dove in after a woman you didn't even know. You risked your life to come into that rapid flowing water and pull me out. And not just from the door you went to first, but you had to go all the way around through that rapid rushing water and get to the other door—" she smiled, "and I wouldn't come out, so you reached your hand in and you grabbed my hand. You didn't yank me; you just grabbed my hand and waited for me to come to you. No, you never did what your mom did. And if a woman ever accused you of that, I can guarantee you she's looking for an excuse, some other reason to leave. Honestly, just from what I know about you in the less than a week we've known each other, no one would ever do you wrong."

He couldn't move, just stared at her as her mind-boggling words wrapped around him. In that moment, all he wanted to do was pull her into his arms and kiss her. Kiss her like she'd kissed him the night he rescued her in that deep rushing water. Hold her close and kiss those beautiful lips of hers, feel her arms slide around his neck and pull him close— *No,* his mind screamed. But as he looked at her, in his heart of hearts—as much as he didn't want to admit it, he knew it was true—he wanted to kiss April. But most of all, he wanted to know more about her. To know who she was, get to *really* know her.

* * *

Staring at Chet, April knew it was time to leave. She had opened her big mouth and said far more than she should have. If the suddenly disturbed expression on his face told her anything, it was that. *Was it the same thing she was feeling? The need to kiss her like she was feeling the need to kiss him?* Ridiculous for two people who did not want anything to do with a relationship. *What was she thinking?* She stood. "Okay, I'm finished. I think my clothes are probably dry. And look out there—I see a little twinkle of sunshine. It's stopped raining. So, we better get on our horses and head back before it comes again." She'd left her phone in the bathroom, so she had no idea whether the rain was coming back, but it was time to go.

Chet stood, looking calm and agreeable. "I'll get your clothes. Then we'll ride back to the stables a little faster to see how you can ride on a horse that is calm but enjoys a little fast trip every once in a while." He started toward the dryer, then turned back to her. "I'm not going to let you get hurt. I'll get you back safely." And then he headed to the laundry room.

She stared after him. If her thoughts were right, he wanted to get rid of her as much as she wanted to get gone. Sure enough, thankfully, her clothes were dry. She took them from him, being careful not to touch him, then changed in the bathroom, grabbed her phone and stuck it into her back pocket and headed out to find him. He was waiting at the front door with his boots on and his cowboy hat—a dry hat, sat on his head. She sat on the now-dry bench, pulled on her not-completely dry boots, then rose. "I'm ready."

"Sorry the boots aren't completely dry. The heat in that boot warmer dried them some but by this weekend they'll be better. But don't wear them much so they'll be ready for all the dancing you're going to do at the reunion."

"I'll do that. I actually love these boots—I don't want to ruin them. All right, let's go." She didn't hesitate, and he had already opened the door. The horses were waiting and ready, and she didn't stop as she strode straight to the horse, grabbed hold of that saddle horn, stuffed her boot in the stirrup, and lifted herself up. She grinned as she threw her leg over the horse and settled in the saddle. Unable to stop herself, she looked at Chet.

He grinned.

"You did that good—you're a quick learner."

And then she watched as he practically hopped on the back of the horse in one motion and led the way. They didn't talk much on the way back to the barn. She didn't mind because the more they talked, the harder it got to understand what in the world was going on between them.

When they got back to the stables, lo and behold, there were the boys. Some of them were outside the barn, throwing ropes at a fake cow horn or cow thingy they practiced their roping on—she was going to have to ask and get the name right. And then, as they rode up, the little one, Sammy, jogged up toward them, B.J., the little bitty one, right behind him. "Hey there, cowgirl!

So you ready? We knew you had to have a little practice and we hated when the rain came. We were really worried but Miss Jolie, she assured us that you would be okay, that you were with Chet and he wouldn't let nothing happen to you and we knew that, so yay."

B.J. stepped up, beaming. "I told him you'd be okay, that you were going to be a good horse rider and you were on my favorite horse right there, that nothing would happen to you when you were on that cutie pie." He petted the horse's nose; the horse stuck her tongue out and licked him in the ear. B.J. busted out laughing. "She likes me, she likes me a lot. But I'm not going to lick her, even though I like her a lot too."

She laughed, and so did Chet as the other boys reached them.

"Here, take my hand," Tony said as he reached her, lifting his hand up to her.

She had loved listening and watching the boys. She hadn't dismounted and smiled at Tony as he lifted his hand up to her. He wore a short-sleeved T-shirt—she hadn't seen him in short sleeves before, and she was startled to see his arm. She saw scars. Scars she had heard about. She didn't let her eyes linger—no, never. This boy was much more than scars. He was an amazing boy. And one thing was for sure—if he stayed here and did as good a job as she was certain Chet was doing, then Sunrise Ranch was going to be in good hands.

They had gotten off the horses and she was talking to the boys when Nana stuck her head out of the kitchen.

"Hey, come on in here. My daughters-in-law are here. I want to introduce you."

Chet grinned at her. "Go on. You already met Suzie. Now you get to meet Lucy and Jolie."

She loved that no one hesitated, thinking that she wouldn't like them or that they wouldn't like her. She headed that way in her still slightly damp boots, her dry jeans, and her blow-dried hair.

"Hi. It's really good to see you again," she said as she reached Nana.

"I'm really glad to see you. And I'm hoping you had a good time out there with Chet."

"I did. We had a great trip. Y'alls ranch is beautiful and well, uh, we had an experience. You know…it rained."

Nana laughed and waved her inside.

She entered and there, from the kitchen, she could see two women talking as they worked on something on the counter. Nana didn't say anything else; she just followed her in. And as soon as she entered the kitchen area, both gals quit what they were doing, which looked like decorating cookies.

"Hi there. I am Jolie. I am the kids' teacher and

married to Morgan, and we are so glad to meet you."

"And I'm Lucy. I'm married to Rowdy, and I'm glad to meet you, too. We all love Chet, and we're very thankful that he saved you that night. We all knew he was a hero already—he's so good with all the boys— but he actually got to be a hero to you that night and we're thrilled."

"Well, I'm so glad he was there, too, and yes, I agree with y'all—he is a hero. And I have to tell y'all, this ranch is wonderful. I got an urge to come here after reading an article about the ranch."

She had almost said *a letter from Mabel*; she was going to have to watch that. After she got the letter, she had researched it; she had read articles about the ranch and wanted to come. She couldn't give in that it started with a letter from Mabel to B.P. Joel.

"We're excited you're here and I'm just going to tell you," Jolie said, "the boys are looking forward to you going on the cattle drive on Friday. We've all been on one of those cattle drives and they're fun. We could come along, but the boys love meeting new people and showing them their experiences, so you're going to have a great time. Also, I hear you're a writer for articles of some sort. Are you researching for an article? A story?"

"So what are y'all doing?"

Nana picked up a cookie. "We're baking cookies,

getting ready for the festival we're having this month. We make them early and then we freeze them. We're able to take them out and thaw them right before everybody gets here. But if we try to do everything that we do for the reunion that weekend, we'd never get it done."

"We do what Nana says. I'm not a great cookie maker," Jolie said, "but I make her recipe, and I've learned to use a cookie cutter pretty good. As a kayaker, I haven't had to use my hands for this sort of thing much but I'm learning."

Lucy handed her one. "Enjoy! They're good. And she's right—she's doing a great job. Me, not so sure, but I do whatever these wonderful gals tell me to do."

"I heard that you're an artist and you do a wonderful job, just like you're a kayaker and were great at what you did do or did—well, I mean, the boys were telling me all about it."

She took a bite of the cookie; it was so good. She looked at Nana. "I could eat a bunch of these without any icing on them. Amazing."

"Thank you very much. I like cooking, just like my daughter-in-law did, before she passed away. We'd get in here…well, at that point, we were in our kitchen at the house. She left more than a wonderful memory for her family, for us…her friends, and her husband and sons. She left a feel of her presence in the food she loved and the lives she continues to touch." Nana's eyes teared up. "And I'll always be grateful she loved my son with all of her huge heart and passed that love to my grandsons and now to all these precious people we call ours." She looked around the room at her grandsons' wives, and April felt the love and saw it in the way they all looked at Nana.

By the time April headed to the hotel, she was in a daze. She'd never seen someone leave this world and touch so many lives day after day through the love she continued to bring through the friends and family who loved her.

Then again, as she walked into the diner, her thoughts flashed back to the horrible moment she met her dying daddy's gaze as he pulled that trigger and saved her life. Tears filled her eyes. He'd loved her. Her mother too. So much so that they'd given up the life they'd known, thinking they were protecting her. And then they'd given their lives, trying to save her... In that moment, she remembered her mother pushing her toward the door right before she was shot—she'd been trying to save her too. And all these years, her anger and pain had hidden that from her. She'd been too torn up and only saw what they hadn't given her.

CHAPTER FIFTEEN

Rowdy looked at Chet. "So, is April going to go with us? The fellas think she is, and they seem really excited."

Tucker nudged him with his elbow. "Are you excited?"

He looked from his two brothers to his oldest. Morgan must have stared at him, his lip hitched up on the right side. "Well? I hope she's going. And I believe that interest I see in your eyes might be real. It'd be about time."

"Guys, come on. Don't push this. Y'all know I'm not interested."

"You can say that all you want." Rowdy grinned, his eyes sparkling. He was the mischievous one of the four of them, and that had gotten him into trouble in his early life. But he had lived through it and was now one of the happiest people Chet knew.

"I can. Look, I took her riding. She did good, so even if the horse starts running, I think she'll ride him well. And since we're not going as far down the river as we sometimes go, I think she's safe." He sealed his lips, not going where they wanted him to go.

Tucker crossed his arms and his expression got serious. "Come on. If you don't open up, you're going to live your life alone. And I can tell you—I was in your position, maybe not for the same reasons—but I can promise you, you'll want to open up. I'm the happiest man I've ever been since I met Suzie and Abe, and if I'd have kept myself closed up, I would've never known what I know now. You need to know that, little brother—you need to open up."

Chet knew what Tucker had been through, the hardship, and his words dug deep inside him. There was this want, this need that he was determined to deny— but why? If they all could be happy after suffering what they had suffered, why couldn't he let himself be happy? April's beautiful face appeared in front of his gaze: her smile, her glistening dark hair with that shimmer of red-golden hint, and those eyes...those gorgeous golden eyes. He wanted to tell his brothers that he was going for it, all in. Instead, he shook his head and headed toward the door.

"I have to go check the cows. Talk to y'all later. See you on Friday." And then he walked out front, hopped into his truck, and headed toward a pasture far away from here, all the way on the other side of this large ranch. He needed to not have anybody looking at him; he needed to get his head on straight, because all he had thought about all night long was April and that determination of her own to not get involved with him.

And then there were her words. The way she said things sounded familiar. Something deep inside him said April was hiding something. There was this need inside him to know what it was that drove her.

He was going to stand back, do what she wanted and not intrude because, just like him, she didn't want a relationship, had made it clear that she wasn't going there. So why was he determined to keep thinking that if he was going to have a relationship with anyone, she was the one?

* * *

April had awakened on Friday morning excited about riding horses—well, herding cattle with those boys. She was not thinking about Chet. Of course, that was a lie. She had thought about the man a lot, but today she was thinking about getting to ride horses with these boys who seemed so excited about having her on the trail with them. Plus, she was really interested in learning about how to herd cattle. It would work great in one of her books. She didn't like the idea of a horrible killing like usual would happen in the book and her suspect would be a cowboy—no, that did not feel right. The cowboy would have to be her hero. The hero of the book, not her hero.

There was just something wrong. In her usual conception of her books, she always had the bad guys and she always saved the day—not her, but the character she wrote about. The character who had some of her in it, but was not her. For some reason, she always thought about that psychologically, yes, it was her really, but she didn't like to admit it. She kept thinking about Chet and what he had said about her book. And not just what he had said, but what Mabel had said. Did everybody who read her books think that the author had placed herself in them as the main character?

She tried to push the thoughts away as she drove to the ranch. She was going to have a great day; she was going to learn from the experience, and she was going to enjoy these boys who had survived their early life, not just having no parents but many, like Tony, survived horrifying experiences—like her. Yes, she had been lied to by her parents her entire life, even though she now knew it was for her own protection and it was a miracle that she had lived through what had killed her parents. The miracle being that, before he took his last breath, her dad had managed to save her.

She parked the SUV as that thought lingered. Her father had held on long enough to save her, and yet she always resented him not telling her that she was living a fake life.

Enough, she yelled inside her mind as she opened the SUV door and stepped into the sunshine. The sunshine she much needed.

Cupcake whinnied at her, already standing beside the fence, saddled and ready. Several of the boys stood beside their horses, grinning as they talked and laughed. Over to the side, Sammy and B.J. were practicing roping a fake cow, tossing ropes, and she watched as B.J.'s rope sailed through the air and landed around the fake cow's neck.

The boys instantly grinned and slapped their palms to each others in a high five.

Tony's yell of congratulations from where he stood with the other guys, including an older man she hadn't met yet, made her and the older man smile. Her thoughts instantly went to the scars she'd seen on Tony's arms.

The physical and mental trauma he must have lived

through was far worse than what you've been through. The words reverberated through her. Her parents had never done anything but...protect her. The truth slammed into her. *They just hadn't saved themselves.*

Several of the boys headed her way, she knew she wanted to know each of their stories. Why, she wasn't sure. But what she was sure of was she loved seeing the smiles on their faces. She wanted to know who they really were, what they lived through to become or were on their way to being amazing, wonderful men. She wanted to help them any way she could. The very idea spun through her like dancing sparkles, igniting something inside her she suddenly knew was not going to go away.

If she knew something about them, could she help them?

Could she be part of this wonderful operation that rescued them and made them smile again?

The question was, how could she help?

"Hey there, April," Tony called, striding toward her. He had a white T-shirt on. His wavy, dark hair stuck out from his straw hat that was not a new hat—it looked as though it had been through a lot.

The boy was smiling that Elvis-tilted smile with those eyes dancing and sparkling in the sunlight. Her heart roared with joy seeing that smile and after knowing his past. And knowing he wanted to help everybody else.

He halted a few feet from her. "We're glad you made it. Are you ready?"

"I can't wait. And I see y'all got my little horse all saddled up for me. Thank you."

To her surprise, he wrapped an arm across her shoulders, didn't hug her; just pulled her in so their shoulders touched. "You're welcome." Then he let go and hiked a brow. "The boys are so excited to have you on the trip. It's just going to be a great day."

She was surrounded now.

"We're glad you're coming with us." Caleb's eyes twinkled. In his hand, he held a screwdriver and in his other hand, he held what looked like something from an engine—she wasn't really sure.

"I'm excited, too, but I'm curious...what do you have in your hand?" She looked around as all the guys laughed and he grinned.

"I'll fess up—I have this tendency to take things apart. This came off one of the tractors. I'm going to put it back on but I'm just taking it apart and seeing how it's made."

"He does things like that all the time, and every once in a while," B.J. looked at Caleb, then pushed him in the waist and laughed. "He doesn't get all the parts put back in and it can cause problems."

"I'm going to get it back on—just wait."

She smiled. "I'm sure you'll do great. I guess that's how creative minds work. You have to learn as you go. I think that's cool your curiosity makes you take things apart and put them back together."

Micah chuckled. "I'm always impressed by what he does. He made this thing—well, we'll have to show it to you. It's in the work barn. He took an old office chair and removed the back. You don't sit on it—you lay your stomach on it. Then you hold your legs out and pick up the gas leaf blower, turn it on and take a ride."

"Yes, around and around," Sammy yelped as he and everyone laughed, including April as she pictured the boy spinning on the chair seat from the pressure of the air like a small airplane.

Caleb grinned. "It's fun. The air pressure spins you round and round. And then you turn it on and point it at the ground then the circles begin—on concrete, that is. It's a blast—seriously. It's kind of like making your own ride at an amusement park. We all like to do it. Sometimes it's a disaster, like one time I somehow made it blow really strong and it blew me off the little concrete slab, so I *flew*. I flew off the concrete and got dumped across the gravel." He grinned. "I had a few scars but when they all saw I was okay we laughed forever. But I don't think you want to have that kind of fun so if he asks if you want to do it, just say no."

Everybody was laughing as Chet came up, grinning too. "We never know what to expect from Caleb. We're watching to see where his curiosity takes him."

"He'll be an astronaut maker," B.J. said. "You know, the one who makes the spaceships that go up in the air."

"Yeah," Sammy agreed. "I see him doing that too."

Caleb laughed. "I might want to do that, but I don't know if I want to build a spaceship or fly it. I don't even know if I'm smart enough to build a spaceship."

"Time will tell. You're in school—work your hardest," she said. Writing hadn't come from hard work on her part but from need. From a deep down need to get her emotions on paper. It had been her way of hiding her pain, hiding feeling out of focus after losing her parents and finding out that she had never known who she really was. She had become driven and the writing had come naturally, so who was she to say that somebody had to work hard at class to be good? She had barely even known she was in class she was so lost for so long. But right now, she threw all that aside and focused on the boys, not herself.

"I can tell you..." Chet said. His gaze met hers,

sending her stomach rolling like she was caught in a huge ocean wave and wishing she hadn't met his gaze. "They're excited you're here, and we're going to have a good day."

"Yes, we are," said a tall, black-haired man with a touch of gray at the edges.

There was another older man about the same age who came up to stand beside Chet. Three other men came along with them and they looked more around Chet's age.

"I'm Randolph McDermott," he continued. "These are my sons, Morgan, Rowdy, and Tucker. And this is my top ranch hand, Walter Pepper, one of the best men around. We're glad to meet you." All of them had pulled their hats off when introduced and each shook her hand.

"Yes, we are, and call me Pepper," the white-haired older man said, taking her hand from Tucker. "Everyone knows me by that name." He shook her hand, grinning as he gave it a welcoming, gentle squeeze before letting go.

"It's nice to meet you, Pepper, and you, Mr. McDermott. All of you. What a great place this is."

"Please call me Randolph, and thank you. We love our camp. Love having this home for all our wonderful boys and young men I call my own. And it was my beloved late wife's idea. She would be thrilled to know you are here and going to experience a cattle drive with these fellas."

She couldn't help staring at him. Her gaze went to the other three men, his sons, standing beside him. Two, Rowdy and Morgan, were muscled and lean, pure cowboy material with their black hair and tanned faces like their dad. The third man, Tucker was larger, hugely muscular and had beat everyone taking his hat off when they'd walked up.

Now he spoke since they'd allowed their dad and Pepper to talk first. "Suzie is my wonderful wife and she told me who you were at church. We were a long distance and didn't interrupt everyone else meeting you that day."

"She's as beautiful and sweet as all those flowers she is surrounded by." His grin widened.

"I totally agree."

"I'm Rowdy—as Dad told you. My wife was really thrilled to meet you the other day and told me the boys had invited you along today. Of course, we all heard about you from them at breakfast, lunch, and dinner." The cowboy chuckled and his eyes danced as he glanced at all the smiling boys.

"Your wife is lovely and I'm more than happy to be

going on this ride now than ever."

"You'll love it. They're great fellas and yes, my wife is lovely. And the boys say you are too, and you're living up to their praise."

"How sweet," she said, awed by the boys' praise of her to everyone.

Then the one she'd heard so much about, Morgan, smiled. He looked almost identical to his father despite the age between them. This was the man all the kids looked up to as one of their main leaders and a brother. The man who helped and would one day take over the kids' program. "The boys have spoken highly of you as has my wife, Jolene. You'll have a great time today. These fellas know what they're doing and I'm happy they want to show you what they love."

Randolph stepped up at that. "That all true, now I'm heading to my office—just wanted to welcome you and say have fun. These boys do know what they're doing and they love it. My mother, Nana, will be along to feed everyone at noon. That's her calling and no one can outdo meal cooking on these roundups, so enjoy."

"I'm overly excited now, and am delighted the boys asked me to come along. Thanks, fellas."

To that she got whoops and so many up in the air hand slaps that she was laughing so very happily, but about that time a chuckling Morgan took over.

"Okay, y'all ready?" he asked and got more boisterous yells of "let's do it" as they headed for their horses. Morgan looked at her. "Now that all of them are tending to business and you can hear me," he smiled and she chuckled, "you'll ride beside Chet. He'll make sure that you're safe. We don't want a cow or a calf getting carried away and stirring up your horse or anything like that. Though Cupcake is a great horse, we know from experience first riders need someone by their side just in case we have surprises. We don't want you getting hurt."

She wanted to say she didn't want to ride by Chet, but she knew that wouldn't be good. She looked at him, the man who had been quiet while everyone talked and now she realized he looked like he wasn't any happier than she was about riding beside each other.

Well, at least they were in agreement. But they had boys who would be watching so she plastered on a smile. "I'm ready when y'all are."

Morgan looked from her to Chet then grinned. "Then let's get this roundup going."

CHAPTER SIXTEEN

Chet had fought off telling Morgan, *"No, she's riding by you,"* but he'd managed to keep his mouth shut. He saw in Morgan's grin that he knew there was something going on.

There was no denying that there was. And his brothers had probably all figured out that they were right about his attraction to this beautiful woman. And after being introduced to her, they could all tell why. She was wonderful and he needed to get over this draw to her.

Maybe riding beside her today would help.

Maybe it would help satisfy that want that he had known was there to get to know her better.

Maybe it would give him a chance to drill deeper into who she was and why she'd said the things she'd said. Then again, maybe out here with all these boys swarming around, that might not be a good thing.

He led the way to their horses as all the boys were hopping into their saddles, ready to ride and grinning as they watched him and April. Yep, he and April were the science project today, under the microscope and going to be observed from all angles. He rubbed his forehead and tried to prepare himself. He couldn't mess up.

He untied their horses and looked at her. "You want me to hold onto the reins or do you think you'll be fine on your own?"

She reached for the reins. Her fingers touched his and instantly sent sparks flying through him. It was a *mere* short touch because she yanked the reins away in a flash, still it raced through him.

"I'll take them," she said, in almost a gasp. "You know I can get on this horse all by myself. But thank you very much."

He watched as she did just that and he tried not to feel anything or have any emotion written on his face, because he knew there was a whole herd of boys watching. He felt every pair of eyes on him and April. It was like squirrels eyeing acorns they had plans for. But not just the boys' eyes but Morgan, Rowdy, and Tucker too.

Thank goodness in that instant Nana walked out of the kitchen, carrying something she was loading onto the food truck. "Good morning," she called, all happy and excited as she placed it into the back seat what he could see now were cooking tools.

"Good morning," April said happily. Probably as relieved to see Nana as he was.

Nana grinned. "I made a really delicious dessert I hope you'll enjoy at lunch. I know these boys will. I've got tea and water and barbeque on buns. On short trips like this, I prepare it beforehand, and since this is just a day trip, that's what I've done. If it were an overnight trip, I'd do like the old days and cook it on-site somewhere out there on these acres, with many a past history of ancestors doing exactly the same thing. Of course, I'm a little more advanced with my souped-up truck, a modern-day chuck wagon."

That got laughter from everyone.

"It's awesome, Nana," B.J. called.

"I'm excited about the trip and can't wait to eat your food, and dessert after enthusiasm like that." She smiled at cute B.J., and he grinned back.

Within minutes, they were riding in the opposite direction that she had ridden with Chet. Tony led the way; he leaned down and opened all the gates, then headed for the next one. Micah seemed to be the oldest, and he helped Morgan and Rowdy watch the edges of the boys, making sure everything was good. Chet and

April followed everyone. Maybe from back here no one would notice the tension radiating between them.

* * *

"We're going to stay back here and you can watch," Chet finally said and April glanced at him. The strain between them was rough.

"And participate too, since there will be cows that break out and need to be moved back in line. But the boys really love doing this and will be showing off for you today, so this will give you a better view."

"These boys are so wonderful. I'll enjoy watching them."

"I'm sure you will. Now, we'll stay on this side of the cattle, away from any water's edge. Just to be safe."

She didn't want to be a coward but she had no desire to be near the water right now. She hoped that didn't stick with her, that the traumatic experience of getting washed off that bridge didn't always stay with her. She had enough nightmares' from the past that she'd managed to work through so she knew she wasn't a chicken. She just didn't want to risk something happening in front of the boys.

Once again, her mind filled with all the years she had been living alone, never settling down. Never getting to really know anyone. And now as she rode she knew she was surrounded by people she wanted to get to know better.

She looked at Chet and of course her stinkn' pulse raced. He was riding with one hand—wrist, actually—resting on the saddle horn, and the other lay on top of that hand with the reins in them. She tried not to stare at the man but couldn't help it. Then his gaze shifted from watching the boys ahead of them to her. Embarrassed, she stared straight in front of her, knowing that he probably thought she was studying him with a heartthrob—which it was.

"You're riding good," he said, as if knowing the tension had to ease up. "You take to things pretty easy, it seems."

She kept her eyes focused forward, not wanting to look at him directly just in case there was anything he might see in them that she didn't want him to see. "Yes, I am. I've never really gotten involved in anything like this growing up, so I had no idea. But I really enjoy it."

"You kept to yourself?"

"Yes, I did. I've always kept to myself. *I* was in foster care, but it wasn't like this." There she'd admitted it. Her gaze slid to him and he looked taken aback by her admission. "It wasn't like I was really their child, and I didn't want to be. I had memories of my parents that I couldn't give up despite the pain of realizing I had no idea who I really was. Then, well…" She suddenly wanted to tell him that her parents had lied to her all the time she had known them. Nobody was around them; everyone was ahead of them and here they were, basically alone back here in the wide pasture, heading toward one that must have cattle. But right now, it was just them trailing everyone. She glanced at him, and he was still riding casually, those amazing blue eyes of his studying her.

"You can tell me," he urged, his tone gentle.

"Okay," she said, strain in her eyes. "We were talking the other day, and I got up and left because my mom and dad never told me that we were in protective custody, hiding out using a fake name. Yes, I was raised under a fake name, which is now my real name. And I only learned that after they were dead."

"What?" He looked dumbfounded.

"Exactly. The man who shot and killed them was the man they had sent to prison. He escaped, found them—I don't know how and have never been able to find out. But he found them and killed them."

"Wow, April, I'm so sorry," his gentle words dug deep.

"Me too. But if it wasn't for my dad lingering, hanging on long enough to lift his gun and shoot the man who was about to kill me, then I wouldn't be here either," her voice trembled. Never had she admitted this or told anyone. "So, yes. I was saved by my dad and only after he closed his eyes and died did I find out that I knew nothing about my real identity—who I really was. Nothing." She inhaled and wanted to turn the horse and gallop the opposite direction.

"And I thought I'd been through a terrible trial losing my parents. They weren't murdered for obviously doing something good." He reached out and let his fingers brush her arm. "How did all that come about?"

The soft sway of the horse beneath her had a soothing rhythm and she was glad. She needed something other than the gentle touch of Chet's fingers against her skin. A touch that could dig deeper than she needed it to. *Focus, April.*

"I looked it up when I was older, and my dad had no one in his family—my mom either. It was like they'd been drawn to each other because they were each alone. And then they witnessed a killing when I was a baby and went into protective custody… And then they died and I had no one. So, my world churning like a cement truck full of boulders, I went into foster homes. They were so different than this. Than Sunrise Ranch. The McDermotts—and you, too—have done an amazing job. I've never seen anything more wonderful. And you agree with that, don't you?"

"Yes, I agree one hundred percent. I'm so sorry about your past. That's why I'm going to be here and help out. Yes, I'm paid and I could go out and get a job doing this or in business, which my degree is in. I could do anything, or raise cattle on my own farm…probably enjoy it. But no, I'm going to stay here. I love it. This is where I belong."

Unable to stop herself, she smiled—a wide, full smile. She'd known that was what he would say. "And you're good for the boys. I see it. It's undeniable." As she said the word that so described him, it hit her that, yes, he was an undeniable cowboy, a cowboy through and through.

And just a wonderful person determined to help others who went through something similar to what he went through. In her heart of hearts, she admired him, everything about him. The man had saved her, and he was on the determined path to help save boys who had been through similar things before they were sent to this amazing ranch.

She realized they were still traveling on their horses but they were staring at each other.

In that instant, she wanted with all of her heart to reach out and give him a hug. She remembered how secure and safe she'd felt when he'd pulled her from that sinking, waterlogged car and saved her life in that raging river. She forced her gaze away, fighting off the emotion but couldn't deny that she wanted to be in his arms again.

She was in trouble.

CHAPTER SEVENTEEN

Chet's heart pounded at what she'd told him. She'd been in protective custody and her dad had saved her life. Unlike her, he'd known who he was. He'd known his real name. He'd known and loved his parents and lost them in the midst of a family falling apart. But she had been loved by her parents, protected by them in protective custody after they'd stood up and put someone in prison, who obviously needed to be there. And then he'd been set free or escaped—he missed that part in his processing of her story. The man had found them and killed them, but thank goodness her dad had lived long enough to save her life.

Tears welled in his eyes and he looked away at the very idea of what she'd lived through, but especially of what that poor man had gone through, who'd done the right thing and then found himself on the ground dying with his wife and about to watch his sweet little daughter die too. *Horrible.*

Everything in Chet hurt. He didn't want to imagine the emotions her dad had felt. He was thankful that her dad was able to hang on long enough to kill the thug so that she could live. But with everything she had to learn at such a young age, of course she would still be scarred by it—*scared* by it. Especially a young kid. In many ways that she might not even realize.

As much as he had always kept his heart to himself, his heart was suddenly swelling with the need to take this woman in his arms and tell her that he…*what?*

You know what.

He glanced back at her. She was now looking straight ahead as they'd both started to move their horses forward. Like they both needed to do, he realized like a kick in the chest.

He needed to move forward.

He needed to admit he loved her.

He loved her.

How had that happened in just barely over a week? It was as if it were meant to be. He'd been there when her car had been swept down that hill into that river, and if he hadn't gotten to her, she would have died in that water.

He closed his eyes for a moment as that sank in. There had been no way out. And now, he—the one who saved her, the one who was determined to keep his heart to himself so that he could be here for these boys who had been through similar things as he had—was staring at a beautiful woman who had suffered through far more than he'd ever experienced. Yes, he'd suffered that moment and later, but he'd adjusted. It hadn't been easy but at least he'd known who he was. As much shock as he'd been in hearing his parents fight and moments later, they were over that bridge and gone and he'd never seen them again. He'd known he would have been facing sadness no matter what happened. But he knew as much as he'd loved them, he loved this sweet, wonderful lady more. With all of his heart.

She'd been a poor kid who'd watched her mom and dad murdered in front of her by the hideous man, and then he came after her. His heart pounded and his mind reeled. He had to fight his hands from reaching across the small space between their horses, wrap his arms around her and pull her over onto his lap and hug her tightly…and to tell her he loved her.

He. Loved. Her.

He had to tell her he would always be by her side, God willing.

Now he just had to figure out what to do. He knew

right now he needed to tred easy. Because she was determined to ignore it, hide behind her travels and articles, just go to a new town and stay for a short while and then leave, just like she was going to do here.

But could he stop her?

Could he let her go?

No.

In that moment, he knew there was no way he could watch her go. He had never planned to fall in love. Never. But he now realized when you fell in love, it wasn't something you could stop. And he also knew he'd never been one to walk away from something. He looked at her again. Thank goodness his eyes were dry as reality set in, making him realize that, yes, he loved her but there were a lot of things to overcome for that love to ever be expressed. If he expressed it right now, he had a feeling she would get in her new shiny SUV and be gone. Never looking back. He couldn't have that.

But what could he do?

As he rode, he looked down at his hands and said a prayer. He needed guidance and help. If this was God's plan, he needed a miracle.

* * *

They had gone through another gate, and April saw the

cattle down a hill. She heard the *whoop whoop, whoop* as the boys all yelled out and sped their horses up. She saw Morgan take the lead. Rowdy stayed on the right. And the older boys were on the right side too, while the younger boys were on the inner side where she and Chet were. Abe, Tucker's stepson, rode near B.J. and they were the closest to them.

She looked over at Chet for the first time since she had had a very strong notion that she had said too much. Thank goodness they had something different to talk about now. "So am I imagining it, or is there a reason why the older boys are over there with Rowdy and the younger boys are over here on the same side I'm on?"

There was something in his eyes that hadn't been there before when he looked at her, it was warm and at the same time looked pained. *What was that?*

"Because we are going to be near the river for just a little bit so they're all going to be on that side. We keep the young ones away from the water's edge. They can go into the woods and catch cows or be in here from the back. But that's another reason I'm back here, not just to keep you out of trouble." He smiled and she couldn't help smiling back.

"I get it," she said, so drawn to this protector.

"Tony, Micah, and Jake—the three older ones— they're good. They know what they're doing and even though Jake hasn't been here as long as little B.J. he's good. Like Tony, he took up riding like it was a gift from God. And actually for both of them it has been. Like Micah, Jake keeps his pain locked inside, but like Tony being out here in the pastures with the cattle helps him too. All of the boys deal with their past in their own ways. For Tony and Jake, I think getting through internal trauma was helped by learning to tame wild horses. Rowdy is amazing at teaching that and in learning it both have tamed some of the anger they feel. Rowdy teaches them that to tame a horse, you have to learn patience and understanding and it's helped them. But for Tony it's helped, in other ways too. That kid's probably been through more physical torture than any of them. Emotional, hurtful, and excruciating physical torture, and yet *he's* there for all of them."

"I've noticed that and we've talked about it a lot. Have you stopped thinking that him being here would be a bad thing or are you thinking now it would be good for him?"

"The more I watch him, it's like he was made for it. He's so good with the little kids and even the big ones. Like I said, he helped Jake. There's going to be a lot more after the older ones leave and the new ones come in. We never know if they're going to be young or old. I came in at, well, gosh, I was about twelve when my life fell apart—old enough to understand the stuff that was happening. Old enough to be torn apart by it and angry about everything.

"B.J. came in young and scared. He was so bad when he came into foster care that they put him here immediately. He never, as far as I know, went to any other foster home. But for some reason, they knew he needed people who understood what it meant to not feel loved. He's doing really good now. Just look at how he can ride—he barely rode when he first came. There are so many stories riding out there today. I thought B.J. envied Abe because Abe came here after his dad died in the war and Suzie needed help with him because he was in rebellion. He was about the age I was when I came in. They blamed Tucker but God worked it out. Little B.J. wanted a family like Abe had. Abe now has a new home with his mom and a new dad, Tucker and memories of being loved by his dad. B.J. doesn't have that. Sammy either, and they longed for it. Especially B.J.

"But all those boys out there—they just embraced him, and so did Jolie. I sometimes wondered if maybe she and Morgan might adopt him but this last year— look at him. The kid loves his brothers—he calls them his brothers, calls me his brother—and he loves his house parents. He's adjusted, and I think that Morgan and them are thinking the same thing that I'm thinking—he's fine where he is. He feels love from everybody." He looked at her, his eyes penetrating. "It's wonderful to feel love. It's healing. And if you let go of what's hurting you, it happens more easily."

She stared at him and, unable to stop herself, she pulled her horse to a halt, and he did the same. "Have you done that?"

"Yes, I have."

The way he looked at her and his words...they sounded different than they ever had, and she saw in the depths of his eyes that he meant it. So he stayed here on this ranch for those boys—wasn't getting married but he was okay with that, healed by that strong feeling. She knew in her heart of hearts that he would be a blessing, being here for all these boys just like he already had been. She smiled. There was a pain inside her she didn't totally understand—didn't want to understand—but she kept staring at this amazing man, who chose these boys over everything, driven to help them to make a difference in their lives the way this ranch and all the McDermott family and those sweet ladies in town had helped him.

"You are a wonderful man. You're going to help a lot of boys grow into men—good men just like you." And then she looked away. She barely touched her horse's belly with her heels, and she started to move, thank goodness. She moved the horse a little faster than before. She reached the boys, which was a good fill-in for the space between her and Chet—the space that, as much as she didn't want it to, was disappearing.

* * *

At noon, they reached the pasture where Nana was waiting with lunch. Her cooking truck was parked and ready. She, unlike them, had come up one of the dirt roads that was quicker and easier for a truck but cattle didn't drive trucks. It was great, though, for her to meet them, have lunch set up, and it was a fun time for the boys.

He'd enjoyed watching April as the boys showed off for her. It took the strain from between them after the in-depth discussion they'd shared. As they were dismounting and about to grab lunch, one of the cows got away and Sammy got his lasso spinning above his head, tossed it and it landed around the calf's head. Beaming proudly, he looked right at April and she was smiling and clapping her hands, the reins still held as she clapped one hand onto the side of the one holding the reins.

She smiled beautifully as she looked at him. "Just

look at that sweet boy. He's the one you told me was really in a bad way when he arrived. He's also the one that got caught in the rapids in a kayak?"

"Yes, he was struggling after being tossed away by his parents. Both parents let go of him, and it was hard for him to understand. Well, it's hard for anybody to understand why, but they automatically sent him here, which we're thankful for. He's the one who took that dangerous ride down the river and Jolie saved him. But he's doing great—just watching him throw that rope and catch that cow—it's rewarding to the spirit of this place. Like I said earlier, he's happy now, but I guess you noticed."

"You can't help but notice. I guess the one who seems to, well, I'd say struggle the most right now, would be Micah. And did you say he's going to graduate next year?"

"Yes, there are some of us who come here who have to deal with our past after we're legally able to move forward and be on our own. I found my way to deal with it, and he will too. He's gotten stronger since he's been here, but he has things deep inside. Tony—good ole Tony—has tried to help him and has made a lot of progress with him. They are really good friends and I can assure you that will carry on. Like, for me, Morgan—and also Rowdy and Tucker but Morgan especially—helped me, and I helped Morgan because he had lost his mother. He had dealt with it in a hard, hard way, and I had lost mine, God puts, it seems, the right people into your life when you need them."

"He's put you in their lives."

"Yes, and I'm glad. See there's a difference between all of us who've come to the ranch and found home—Morgan and his brother's mother loved them desperately. Her love was so huge and open, but her dream was to love a ranch full of kids who hadn't known what her kids had known and what she wanted to give, so here we are—all of us who hadn't had the love that woman was able to give from her grave because the people she loved so much wanted to fulfill her dream."

April's gaze had locked with his, and her eyes were brimmed with tears. It was touching, he knew. His voice had teared up. He was a man—a very manly man, he thought. He worked hard at it but there was just sometimes that tears were undeniable. There had been a lot of things in his life that had been undeniable, and as he stared at this woman with tears in her eyes, understanding how this family had fulfilled the dream of the woman they loved—all of them—and her dream was making a difference in a humongous amount of lives.

"You'll see at the reunion how Lydia's dream

touched so many lives. We get together and celebrate her by having a fun, wonderful time. And even though I never met her, I've looked at her pictures and we all get to look through photo albums. The woman could smile. And you should see how she cuddled and hugged her boys all through her life. There's a picture at the end, where in her eyes she knows it's almost there—she knows she's almost about to leave but there's still love in those eyes as she's hugging all three of her sons and she's looking at the man holding the camera, which is Randolph." He couldn't help telling her all of this. It was as if he felt she needed to hear how they all formed a happy family.

She reached out and lay her hand on his. "I would love to look at those pictures." Her voice shook. "I lost my mom and dad in that horrible shooting, but they loved me. I have no pictures left over from it; I have nothing. They didn't send anything with me when they put me in the care of those families. Families that, the more I think about it, didn't hurt me. I know some people are blessed to have what Lydia gave all of you, but some people, like me, I had people who had to have cared to bring me in. But the more I look at it, *I* shut them out. I shut myself in closets—*I* hid. I wrote and filled pages with my emotions rather than letting them out for others to see."

Staring at her now, he knew that's what she did; he felt it deep inside, he could tell. "I searched online, trying to find something you've written, and I found nothing. But I have to say, like I said before, when you talk like that…when you open your mouth and let your background out, I somehow feel like I'm reading a book by you right now." What was he doing? The question slammed through him as alarm flashed across her beautiful face.

Alarm… His brain began rolling, instantly he thought back to the new books by B. P. Joel that had come in. Yeah, he had already read another and started a third one, and they did still somehow remind him of this lost woman, in her way of not connecting. Just like the main character in all those books, Tullie always walked away too. Yeah, sometimes she almost opened her heart but then she slammed it and walked away. His mind rolled, familiar moments jumped forward slamming him to alert. *Could this be!*

He continued to stare at her. *No way—but…* She blinked and looked away again, and then took such a deep breath and he could see the tension in her jawline. In the eyes that had gone on alert before dodging away and he knew now that what he'd said had done this to her.

What he'd said—a "April, are *you* B.P. Joel?" Now

more than ever he knew the author's words sounded like April. B.P. could be a woman and he'd assumed it was a man. But now, by the sudden startled frenzy going on in those beautiful golden eyes he no longer thought he was crazy. "You *are* aren't you?"

CHAPTER EIGHTEEN

S he wasn't a liar. She'd never had to bluntly lie about who she was. No one had a clue until now. Here she was, sitting by this beautiful creek—it was peaceful, easygoing, and enticing with its soft sound pulling her in, telling her to tell the truth.

She was beside this amazing man, and he knew who she was. Or thought he did. He saw her in her books. *Oh, how had that happened?*

She wanted to say, *No, that wasn't me.*

But as she lifted her gaze to his, she nodded. His eyes flared and for a moment, she thought he was going to reach for her and pull her into his arms. But then he paused and put his hands back on his thighs and looked out at the water.

She looked there, too, and behind them, above the

beating of her heart, she could hear the boys laughing as they ate the delicious Mud pies that Nana had made, and oh, it was wonderful. She had half of it on her plate and knew that it would never be finished because her stomach was so upset she couldn't eat. She couldn't look at Chet now.

"I started writing that character in closets. Tullie gave me an escape. At first, it was just a way to get away from reality and fighting off the demons haunting me. I had no idea my character was going to become the star of a best-selling series. I just wrote my emotions in the pages of my notepads, pretending it was someone else hurting and it was me solving *their* problems, while mine remained unsolvable. My brain caught on and I began pumping out short tales of rescue and it gave me relief." She looked at him, her eyes deeply troubled. "I was in a lot of pain and couldn't tell anyone. Couldn't express it. But it came out in my words. And then I was about fifteen when the first real idea of a book came to me, and I wrote the book and Tullie solved the mystery. It wasn't a short story, it was a novel. And I became obsessed with it, I was in English class and being taught the right way of doing things so I worked on the book while working on my structure. And Tullie was the heroine solving the victims' families loss so they could heal after the pain of losing their loved one in the book."

She bit her lip, moistened it, and wanted to cry.

"That sounds good. You were dealing with it in your own way."

His words hit the mark. "Yes, I was the one who went in and caught the bad guy or woman. I was the one who solved the problem and yes, because my first editor told me I needed to add a little romance to the book, that even just a little would help sales—I wasn't interested in it but I had to create a character who would be interested in my main character, Tullie. But giving her a romance was as far as I would go, in the end, she always walks away and the publisher accepted that. Like Tullie, I never allowed myself or wanted to let myself be near enough to anyone that I couldn't walk away. So I've never been close to anybody. I keep my distance." She swallowed hard, her gaze drifting down to her hands that were clutching each other.

He wondered whether maybe this was her first time to ever feel anything. Because he wasn't stupid, and he knew what he saw in her eyes sometimes when she looked at him was the same thing she saw when he looked at her. The woman he loved, the woman he now knew could walk away. But he couldn't rush. He was thankful that she would be here for at least the next two weeks.

"You are an amazing author. I don't know if you've

figured this out, but I feel like in your writing, you're helping those like me who, in some way, have some kind of pain that they can't completely get rid of. They attach to your characters and they ride the wave with them. And even though the main character walks away, someone in that book has a happy ending. Maybe not romantic but a problem solved, a new life begins…a good ending."

"I try."

"I'm just going to be blunt with you. I realized while reading the third book that I'm reading—yes, because it speaks to me—but I'm hoping this time by the end of the book Tullie gets her happy ending. I'm sure you know, since you're the author, that they haven't had anything intimate. He kissed her that one time, and you let her have feelings about it. Kind of like that night when you kissed me when I pulled you out of that water. Now I'm wondering if that was an experiment—though you'd already written this book—I wondered if you experienced anything."

She blinked, her eyes glistening as those beautiful golden tones danced in the sunlight. Then she glanced back toward where everyone was; stood and started walking down a trail toward the stream without saying another word. The trail made by cattle when they were here weaving down toward the stream. He stood and followed her down to where the trail met the water. He glanced over his shoulder and saw they were alone and hidden from the camp. He realized it wasn't a romantic thing she'd just done; she, for the first time, was exposed.

And she was trying to deal with it.

"I'm not going to tell anyone," he said, not wanting her to think he would do something she didn't want. "Honestly, you don't have to worry about that."

She turned toward him; her arms were crossed and her hands gripped her biceps. "You're not the first to figure it out. Mabel was the first. She didn't know me when I got here, but she reads my books too and wrote to B. P., using the address where I pick up my mail. Mabel told me about Sunrise Ranch and about the boys. She'd picked up that I had been in a foster home and had not had what these boys had gotten here. Told me not all foster homes were sad. That there were great ones and good ones, and this was a top-of-the-line one and I'd be blessed if I came here and let myself see how wonderful a foster home could be. That they could actually be a home that took them in and gave them a choice before leaving to either remain with their last name or to take the McDermott name. What she wrote me was amazing. Is amazing."

"Yes, it is. I'm one of those who looks at Rowdy,

Tucker, and Morgan and all these boys as my brothers, and Nana as my grandmother, and Randolph and Lydia as my parents now, who I love very much. But my dad, he wasn't the one who wanted the divorce. He wasn't the one who threw his concentration off so bad that he wasn't thinking about the stormy road as he should have been. No, he was thinking about the woman he'd loved telling him she loved someone else and they were through. He lost control and we ran off that road. Because of him I can't give up my last name. But in my heart, I'm still a McDermott, a brother to all my brothers." His voice shook; it was such a deep matter.

As she looked into his eyes, he knew that she saw the emotion there, and before he knew what she was doing, she stepped forward and wrapped her arms around his waist. Instinctively, his hurting heart thundered as he did the same, then pulling her close, he rested his cheek on her hair and breathed in every ounce of her.

* * *

April found herself clinging to him; she hadn't been able to help herself. He had needed this—she had needed this. She had to get a grip. As she told herself that, his arms tightened around her; his chin that was resting upon her head moved and he kissed her on the temple. Everything inside her world shifted. Unable to stop herself, she lifted her head and looked at him, and, as she had kissed him that night he had rescued her, this time, his lips dropped and covered hers.

Unable to stop herself, she reacted to his kiss; everything in her was on high—not alert, as she had felt so many times in her life, but she was sailing on a cloud high above the world. Sunlight like she had never felt before glowed as his lips moved on hers; his arms hugged her close and she felt breathless and in her heart of hearts she knew that she was in love.

Love? No!

Panic, hard and strong, erupted through her. She pressed away from him with her hands. He let her go; his gaze, as if knowing that she was going to do that, studied her. Panic raged inside her. *What had she done?* She couldn't get a word out.

"Stop. Just calm down," he urged gently. "I shouldn't have done that. I know you don't see yourself here, settling down, but, April, you're hiding in your words—you touch people's *lives* with your books. I'm going to tell the boys who are old enough to understand what they're reading, that they should read your books. *Your* books can help some of these boys who are fighting internal emotions, just like Micah. I've already suggested he read your novels, and I gave him your first one. He wasn't exactly thrilled, told me he didn't particularly—well, you've talked to him. He's been thinking ever since that first conversation y'all had—his mind has been whirling. At that point in time, I had no idea that you were the author of the book I gave him. But, he's getting ready to go to college next year, so I decided it was a good message for him so I gave him that book."

"You really did?"

"Yes. I believe that book will touch him. Your *words* are going to move something inside him, maybe help him to see that what he's hiding inside himself could come out on paper and in doing so could help him heal. *You* can help him."

His words touched her so deeply. She wanted to help Micah; she had realized it could help but she hadn't spoken up, she hadn't told him the truth, hadn't suggested he read her book. Staring at Chet, she could believe that he had recognized in her writing what might be able to help Micah.

She blinked away tears, her heart throbbed. "Thank you for that," she managed. "I wondered what I could do to help. My words helped me, but I never thought they could help someone else. It was just my escape and when I sent it in, the editor immediately bought it, and after that, I was still hurting. I was young—I sold my first book when I was eighteen, can you believe that? They didn't know how young I was because I'd aged quickly. My senior English teacher suggested I be a writer, having no idea I'd written that book but that's when I sent it in. But even when it was bought, I had no idea my writing could help somebody else."

He smiled, reached up, and gently caressed her cheek. "Everything about you can help someone. You're just that kind of a person. You immediately took to those boys, whether you knew it or not, and they immediately took to you. It's as if you knew them in a different way than everybody else, in a way that I know them. And a way that I kept feeling like you did too."

She took a deep breath. Everything about this moment hummed through her. Her mind started to whirl; her thoughts combined as words mingling inside started trying to get out—she needed to write.

Needed to go back into her safe place, the place she controlled.

"I'm going to ride back with Nana. I need to go. I need to work. I need to get things out of my head, onto paper. I can't help it—that's the way it is...that's the way it works. Please don't tell anyone what happened between us. I can't promise anything."

She saw the dulling of his eyes as his wonderful lips lifted into a gentle smile. "I know, but I'm going to tell you to go on back and do what you do, because I can already tell you it's going to touch someone. Somehow, God's going to use it."

His words followed her as she rushed up the incline. *God's going to use it.*

* * *

She rode home with Nana, who had asked her if she felt bad. She hadn't lied, just said she didn't feel good. That was true. Nana didn't ask more questions. She got in the truck with her because, while she'd been down by the stream with Chet, Nana had closed up the lunch as everyone else was getting ready to finish herding the cattle. One of the boys was leading her horse in and as they drove away, she didn't look back. She needed to be alone.

Her life was always needing to be alone.

When they reached the house, she was anxious to get inside her SUV and head to the inn. "Thank you, Nana. It was wonderful. I need to get back to town now."

"If you need anything, call." Nana's blue gaze

penetrated her golden eyes.

"I will. I promise." And then, turning, she headed to town.

She went straight to her room. Right now, she was so emotional and exhausted, and her brain was going wild. She would soon be lying on her bed, propped up against her pillows with her computer on her lap. Her computer, the thing that took all her emotions in and made sense of them in the words she typed with fingers full of anger.

This was how her thoughts went. But there was something different about this time, something barreling around in her heart as Chet's words kept flowing through her head. *I can already tell you it's going to touch someone. Somehow, God's going to use it.*

But there were also his other words that clung to her… *I'm hoping this time by the end of the book Tullie gets her happy ending.*

Those words were with her vibrantly, they wouldn't let go, and she didn't know what to do about it.

But the feel of his lips, his arms around her, and the beat of his heart told her what she was trying to deny. Telling her what she most feared of everything…that finding someone meant you could also lose someone—

tears welled in her eyes, in her heart and soul.

She couldn't ever do that again.

Could she?

Her thoughts went to all the boys who had overcome terrible backgrounds of pain and loss. Tony, smiling the Elvis side smile blasted to the front of her mind, sweet, strong, *determined* Tony.

Tony who was determined to follow in his hero, Chet's footsteps… and here she was hiding.

CHAPTER NINETEEN

Chet drove into town. It had been four long days since he had watched April ride away with Nana, and Chet had heard nothing from her. Or anyone. He even asked Nana whether she'd seen her or heard from her, and she'd said no. Mabel said she was being fed, but had asked for time to be alone and work. And they were giving her that time. She had assured him that she was being taken care of—Miss Jo was sending her food and that Edwina—good, wonderful Edwina—was doing a lot of walking across the road, delivering breakfast and a late afternoon meal because she said she didn't need to be disturbed in the middle of the day. She'd also said that she'd opened the door a couple of times and actually seen her but that most of the time there was a note on the door to set it down and she'd get it when she took a break.

A break. She was writing. She'd said her brain was busy, or something like that. He'd been concentrating on the feel of her in his arms and wanting to feel her lips with his again, so he had missed her exact words. But he should have known. Something in her brain clicked, and she was holed up, writing. Or hiding.

As he parked at the diner, he'd wanted to race across the street, storm up the stairs, and bang on her door. When she opened it, he wanted to pull her into his arms and kiss her again, and ask her to give them a chance. To make the dream he'd never wanted to become real. That now he wanted it—her—more than anything he could ever dream of.

But no, he didn't do that. He couldn't do that. Instead, he now walked into the diner, sat down at a table by the window. In the booth next to him sat Chili Crump and Drewbaker Macintosh. They were playing checkers today as their leftover lunch was shoved to the side. Most of the time, they sat on the bench outside, carving little animals or other things they liked to do. But today it was checkers and they instantly started studying him.

It gave him something to talk about and not think about the beauty across the street. "Is your game going good?"

Drewbaker grinned at him. "It's going *real* good. I'm winning."

"Only for a move. I'm 'bout to take him down." Chili shot him a grin.

Edwina came and stood at his table with a stern look in her aggressive eyes. "You don't look so good. You're usually one cute, good-lookin' cowboy when you come in here. But today—oh my, you look like you just ate a terrible, terrible out-of-date pack of salamander or something. What's up?"

He looked up at the woman. She didn't usually question him this much, but there was nothing usual about this woman or this moment. She was highly different and noticed everything. "I'm fine. I'm just, well, worried." His honesty came out, and he couldn't hold it back.

She nodded. "I bet you're worried about our new resident over there that I'm taking two meals a day to."

Bingo. This was the closest person to knowing what was going on with April. "So you're taking her breakfast and an afternoon meal. How is she doing?"

Drewbaker and Chili instantly lost interest in their game as they turned their full attention to his conversation.

"Well, in the last four days, I've taken her things to

eat and in those four days, I've seen her maybe three times. She didn't talk much. She's a friendly person, but I don't know...her gaze is different. She looked like she was somewhere else, she looked so intense. She was nice—she said *"Thank you very much"* and another time she told me, *"I can't wait to eat it"* and this morning she didn't look at me just took the tray and said, *"Coffee,"* then closed the door. That's the only three times I've seen her. All I can say is she's concentrating and when she does that, nothing else is happening."

She was concentrating. "But she looked okay, right?"

Edwina's eyes dug into him, and he saw Drewbaker and Chili concentrate on him too. "Well, she's eating. That's good. When I go to get the dishes, they're almost empty. The question is, how are you doing?"

So, Edwina was asking him how he was doing? The woman saw everything.

As much as he wanted to see April, he knew it was best just to ask and that would let it out...if no one had figured it out already and something about these three faces told him they had. "I need to know—is she okay?"

Edwina looked at him, crunched her lips tight as she obviously debated on what to tell him.

"Go on—give the dude an answer," Drewbaker demanded. "You know me and Chili sit out there on that bench carving and watching everything that goes on in town. And we've seen her up in that room, walking past that window, back and forth. Back and forth. Now, you tell me, if she's writing, is she writing standing up, or does she write the sentence, walk, sentence, walk? Back and forth every other sentence?"

Chili grunted. "That's what we're wondering. You know, everyone is worried about her. Miss Jo is, I think she's back in the kitchen fixing a new coconut pie just for April. And I went out to the ranch to see Nana and I asked her if everything was okay. Because me and Drewbaker have watched this happening every day and it's already in the evening, and you know we're usually already home by now—we do go home, you know. Most of the time we enjoy being entertained by everybody around us. But seeing sweet April up there pacing like that is worryin' us. What do you think?"

They were all three staring at Chet. Edwina was now frowning, Chili's gaze was challenging, and Drewbaker looked as if he were about to give him a thump to the head if his answer was wrong. "I-I don't know. I want to go see her but—"

Edwina stuffed her fists to her hips. "Then *go!* What are you waiting for? *March* yourself across that road and up those stairs and ask that pretty lady what's wrong. But I got a feeling, and I think these two men agree, that you probably already know what's wrong."

He looked at the old fellas. They hitched their bushy eyebrows, and Drewbaker gave his head a nod toward the door and mouthed *Go*.

He looked around the diner and everyone was watching him, and Miss Jo and T-bone stood at the kitchen door grinning.

"Go," Miss Jo said and waved the spatula in her hand at him.

His heart was thundering. They were all right; he did know what was going on. Or he hoped he did. The fact was that he had been always not wanting someone to stay around and want him, and now the thought of her leaving was killing him.

He stood up.

Edwina grinned widely and her eyebrows popped to her hairline as she gave him a shove on the shoulder. Her eyes twinkled. "I knew you would do it. I knew it. I knew it."

The two old guys were grinning too.

Chili chuckled. "Yep, if there's love in the air, take care of it. Don't let it go for years like I have. I know that everyone has figured out that I'm in love with Ruby Ann McDermott...or Nana, as everyone else calls my beautiful Ruby Ann. I've been sending her flowers ever since Suzie opened that flower shop, but Nana hasn't responded like I hoped she would. Oh, she likes getting them—no doubt about that. She's nice to me but she hasn't really given me any indication, other than being friends, that I'm the guy—if there is a guy—who could ever replace her husband Harrison. You know, like Tucker did for Suzie. But I don't know, we've seen you two coming and going a few times since you rescued her. It's only been a little while, but everybody knows there is something going on. We can feel it in the air and see the huge change in you. So, all I can say to you is don't let it go away. From what we hear, she doesn't stay anywhere for long."

"That's right." Drewbaker stood up. "So get up, and walk out that door and get over there. It's a mission—if not for you, then find out what we can do to help her. We don't want her sitting over there suffering…you know, crying because she thinks somebody she loves doesn't love her. Or is it more than that?"

Was it more than that?

Yes, it was. She had always run away from love. She had never really felt it before. He had never felt it before, either, and he was the one who had been—no, he hadn't been running from it. He'd been hiding from it. But in his heart of hearts, he had a feeling that didn't matter. Somehow or other, when the right one came along, God worked it out. The one thing Chet suddenly felt sure of was that if God worked something out for you, you didn't let it go.

He grinned at them. "Thank y'all. You three told me exactly what I needed to hear. I don't need luck—I just need her to love me. And if that's in God's plan, then I'm sure it's going to work out. If not, then I guess I'll live through it." As he walked out the door, he knew people who had heard what he said and knew what was going on were all watching. As he strode across the street, he didn't care whether he was the main attraction. The cowbell had rung as he went past it and he closed the door behind him. He knew if anyone was watching, the three who had encouraged him were. He reached the front door of the inn and to his surprise, a grinning Harvey from the front desk had the door open and ready, and waving him toward the stairs.

"Glad you finally decided to come. That look in your eyes says you are on a mission. Now go on up there, and let's see what happens."

He hoped as he started up the stairs that good things were about to happen. Before he'd taken four steps up the stairs, Mabel stepped out of her office that was near the stairs.

She grinned at him. "I'm glad you're here and that I didn't have to come get you. Third floor, the door at the end of the hall."

He headed up those stairs. He reached the door and paused, then bowed his head and said a quick prayer, though he had a feeling God was already with him. All of this couldn't have happened by accident.

No way could it be an accident. He took a breath, lifted his hand, and knocked.

* * *

April knew he was coming. She'd been at the window when he'd come out of the diner and she'd quickly hidden behind the curtain. She wanted to call out to him, but then saw Drewbaker and Chili at the window, watching him come her way. She had realized from their carving time sitting on the bench that they'd seen her pacing. And now they were watching Chet storm her way with determined steps.

Oh, how her heart was going crazy as she waited, not sure what to do. She wanted him, had fought not to go tell him she loved him. She couldn't chance losing someone she loved again. Her heart ached so much as she stood there and then heard his footsteps, unstoppable as he came her way. Then the knock came.

What should she do? Her mouth was dry and her heart sore, it pounded so hard. She took a step toward the door but couldn't open it.

"I know you're in there. I'm here now and I can't turn and leave again. I have fought this, sweet April with the golden eyes. Eyes that look inside my heart like two hearts of gold that will never let me go. At least, that is my hope, my prayer. I love you, April, and can't *not* tell you."

He paused and her knees weakened.

"April, please open the door and look me in the eyes and tell me if you don't love me. I know you've been so hurt, but I promise, if it's God's will, I'll be by your side for the rest of your life, or I'm praying you'll be by my side for the rest of my life. Either way, we'll know what it is to have someone. Someone who means more to each other than anything...someone to have our own children with, to cherish and love, and never, ever let them not know they are loved. April, please open the door."

Her heart exploded. His words—oh, how the man had a way with words that she'd never expected. Her head reeled from them, and her heart swelled with his words of love and the promise that she would have someone to love, to make up for all the time she hadn't had anyone. She walked to the door but still couldn't open it. Instead, she placed her palm on it and laid her forehead on her hand and took deep breaths.

"I know you're there. I feel you. April, I need you

more than I ever thought possible."

She closed her eyes but felt him through the door. Felt his love and in that moment knew—

"I think you're the bravest woman I've ever known. You have a heart that deals with pain in ways that speaks to those who need you. I need you, but I don't want you to love me just because I need you. I want to give you what you need—love that will never end, arms that will hold you, and a heart that will always beat with you, even if I go before you. I'm yours. I want to be the one at the end of the book who gives Tullie, *you,* your happy ending. Your everlasting love story. The one we build together."

And that was it. Crying, she lifted her head, stepped back, and flung the door open. There he stood—and then he opened his arms. "I love you."

"I love you," she said, throwing her arms around him. "I never let myself say it or think much about it but I hoped to one day have someone in my arms and heart. Tullie always, deep down inside, hoped for the same thing, that happily ever after…"

His smile radiated through her. "I know, and though I can't give it to the imagined Tullie, I've already given my heart to you. Maybe you can give Tullie a happy-ever-after."

She hugged him tighter. "I've been trying to write

it for her but couldn't because I hadn't let myself have it. But now, hers is coming and… well, that's got to happen because though I never knew myself by my real name and never knew it until my parents were gone… Tullie is my real name." Tears filled her eyes. "So you have made all my happily-ever-afters come true."

He pulled her tighter. "Somehow I knew that was really you," he said gently, then kissed her neck. "So my sweet April-Tullie, what name do I get to call you?" Smiling he leaned back to look her in the eyes.

Unable to stop herself she laughed. "April-Tullie it will not be."

They both laughed and then, foreheads together, her heart thundering she whispered, "April. I'll always be both but I've lived my life as April, it means springtime, my mother used to say, Springtime and new beginnings and that I am certain was why when they took me into hiding they gave that name to me. And falling in love with you under that name is me. You are my new beginning. And maybe, when we have a baby, if we have a girl, Tullie can be her name."

"Whatever you want, April, it's my life you've given a new start to. And Tullie gives new hope to those who read about her in your books. I love you, April. And since you mentioned marriage and babies, I hope our new life starts soon." And as his sweet lips covered hers and her arms tightened around his neck and pulled him closer, she knew there could never, ever be a more wonderful happily ever after than this.

Chet was hers, she was his, and together, their dreams could and would come true.

He lowered his lips to hers and kissed her again and as the kiss deepened, her thundering heart grew louder as it pounded against his, the wooden floors even seemed to rattle beneath their feet. Finally she gasped as he pulled away, his eyes holding hers before they both looked toward the stairs, *the stairs*—where the thunder came to an abrupt halt. And there, filling the end of the hallway, stood a bunch of cowboys. Tony was first, Micah and Jake stood behind him and they were all grinning.

She smiled, loving them so much.

Chet chuckled. "Howdy fellas," Chet said. "What's going on?"

Tony's eyes glowed as he snatched his straw cowboy hat from his dark curls. "Well, I have to say, I like what I'm seeing. I actually love it. You two look great together."

"Yep, you do," Micah agreed.

Jake pulled his hat off. "I've been hoping this would happen. I always thought Chet was a smart guy, and this proves it." He smiled and instantly April's tears welled up and flowed down her face.

She smiled at Jake and the other young men who obviously had been rooting for her to wake up and embrace the man they loved and looked up to. "He's also patient and gave me time to come around. I'm so glad y'all made it here to help us celebrate."

Chet's arm pulled her closer to his side. "I'm glad to have y'all on my side. I always knew you were three smart young men, and you knew a winner in April when you saw her. But, something tells my y'all didn't know about us when you came stampeding up those stairs. What's going on?"

They all had their hats off now and like three cowboys waving off a stray cow, they waved their hats toward them.

"Nothing as important as this," Tony was the first to speak. "We just came to say we found your car, April. It's across the pasture where the water expanded from the flood, nowhere near the river now that the water has gone down over there. But it's upside down in the mud and looks awful. We just had to come tell you we found it, and we're glad Chet got you out."

Her heart was full. "Thank y'all for coming to tell me. And as crazy as it sounds, that car and that flood woke me up from a place I needed to be awakened from, a place I needed to leave behind so I could begin again.

After I nearly drowned and this man," she looked up at Chet. "This wonderful man saved me and then all of you," she looked at them. "Helped me see a new life I could begin here. I couldn't be more happy than I am now. I love you all."

She smiled from them to Chet and then as the thundering sound of boots on the floor brought the guys to surround them. She and Chet opened their arms and welcomed the ones they hoped to help find their own healing, hope and, like she and Chet, one day their happily ever-afters.

EPILOGUE

The town was alive with everyone who had come to town for the family reunion. April stood beside Chet, his arm draped around her shoulders as he introduced her to all the guys he'd grown up with. His brothers. His family.

She was so very happy to soon become his wife. And these wonderful people were her family, too. She'd found herself since they'd admitted their love and now were getting ready for a wedding. A month wasn't long, but it gave them time to get things in order and to plan something nice. Chet had told her they weren't exchanging vows in a small group, but with as many who wanted to come or who could come and so, they'd set the date and she had more help than she'd ever imagined helping her prepare. But first was today, watching all the boys who were now men come home to visit and her heart filled to overflowing as she watched man after man walk up and hug Nana, Miss Jo, and Mabel. And some even had hugged Edwina, laughing heartily when she'd threatened to toss them into the water trough at the end of the street.

Edwina, the one who kept to herself but also said what needed to be said when she thought it was needed.

"I wonder if Edwina will ever find love?" she said as she leaned her head against Chet's shoulder.

He chuckled. "I don't know, but she sure straightened me out when I needed her to. What I don't get is she recognizes sincere love and yet she's obviously had a bunch of bad turns for the worse."

"Yes," she looked up at him. "But as we both know, wonderful things can come from the worst. So maybe one day the right man might walk into town and sweep her off her feet like you swept me off my feet."

He laughed, gave her a sweet peck on the lips that sent delight skipping through her. "Darlin', he'd have to figure out a way to bust her feet out of the cement she's stuffed them in, but I can say it would be fun and touching to watch. Or maybe a disaster, so I'm not sure I'm going there. I have enough on my plate watching out for my boys and my soon-to-be bride."

She inhaled and knew she'd made the right

decision. She was marrying this wonderful man, and her last book in her suspense books was coming out and Tullie had found true love and hopefully made more of her readers as happy as it made her and Chet. And now she was starting a new series, romances, because she'd never be able to ever write a book that didn't end with her hero and heroine starting a new and delightfully happy life together.

Even Micah had come and told her he really wanted to see Tullie find love, that he'd been so disappointed in the end of the book, after she'd helped him realize he could have hope and maybe write himself, then she'd walked away. Walked away, he'd said, frowning like she'd just slammed a door in his face. But then, when she'd told him that in the soon-to-be-released book his hope would come true, the young man had busted into a smile, gave her a huge hug, spinning her around then telling her she had been a blessing to not just Chet but to him. He was going to write and no matter what the book dealt with, the one thing that was for certain was it would end with a happy ending. Just like his life was. Oh, he'd said, he still had moments, but he knew he could get through them in time.

And that held her heart, knowing she could help make that happen. Standing there now, surrounded by the reunion of the Sunrise Ranch, all the love that had been found here because of one woman's dream being brought to life by those who loved her gave her strength, hope, and a trust that good could overcome the bad. That joy could come from ashes and that she was living proof, as was Chet and all those she was now calling family.

"I love you, Chet. Thanks for not giving up on me."

He embraced her. "How could I ever do that—you are my everything and always will be.

Now, let's go have some fun. I know some boys are waiting on us competing in the three-legged race. Are you ready?"

"I'm ready. Just hang on and if we fall, let's do it together. And if we fly, we fly together."

"Darlin', you're on. But you know when you get on that chair and hang onto the leaf blower that Caleb has adapted for this day that you'll kind of be on your own."

She laughed. "Oh, that will be fun. You just stand by the side somewhere and make sure I don't hit a ledge and go flying where I'm not supposed to."

"You got it. Now let's go have some fun."

They headed off, arm in arm, and April knew she'd found her place with this wonderful man and everyone here who was now her family.

Her family, oh how happy that made her.

More Books in the Series

Cowboys of Dew Drop, Texas

Unforgettable Cowboy (Book 1)

Unexpected Cowboy (Book 2)

Unlikely Cowboy (Book 3)

Undeniable Cowboy (Book 4)

Undisputable Cowboy (Book 5)

Check out Debra's Other Series

Star Gazer Inn of Corpus Christi Bay

Sunset Bay Romance

Texas Brides & Bachelors

New Horizon Ranch Series

Turner Creek Ranch Series

Cowboys of Ransom Creek

Texas Matchmaker Series

Windswept Bay Series

About the Author

Debra Clopton is a USA Today bestselling & International bestselling author who has sold over 3.5 million books. She has published over 81 books under her name and her pen name of Hope Moore.

Under both names she writes clean & wholesome and inspirational, small town romances, especially with cowboys but also loves to sweep readers away with romances set on beautiful beaches surrounded by topaz water and romantic sunsets.

Her books now sell worldwide and are regulars on the Bestseller list in the United States and around the world. Debra is a multiple award-winning author, but of all her awards, it is her reader's praise she values most. If she can make someone smile and forget their worries for a few hours (or days when binge reading one of her series) then she's done her job and her heart is happy. She really loves hearing she kept a reader from doing the dishes or sleeping!

A sixth-generation Texan, Debra lives on a ranch in Texas with her husband surrounded by cattle, deer, very busy squirrels and hole digging wild hogs. She enjoys traveling and spending time with her family.

Visit Debra's website and sign up for her newsletter
for updates at: www.debraclopton.com

Check out her Facebook at:
www.facebook.com/debra.clopton.5

Follow her on Instagram at: debraclopton_author

or contact her at debraclopton@ymail.com

Made in United States
Troutdale, OR
06/23/2024

20765802R00149